C000132485

YOU TU ... YOUR BACK

YOU TURN YOUR BACK

by

Royston Tester

Tightrope Books
207-2 College Street
Toronto, Onrario M5G 1K3
www.tightropebooks.com

Editor: Sèphera Girón
Typography: Dawn Kresan
Cover design: Deanna Janovski
Author photo credit: Lei Zhao

Printed and bound in Canada

We thank the Canada Council for the Arts and the Ontario Arts
Council for their support of our publishing program.

Library and Archives Canada Cataloguing in Publication

Tester, Royston Mark, author
        You turn your back / Royston Tester.

Short stories. ISBN 978-1-926639-81-9 (pbk.)

        I. TITLE.

PS8639.E88Y69 2014   C813'.6   C2014-907563-4

For Anna Omedes Regàs

Contents

Dotty

Choosing England was her way of saying *I don't care.*

She was going out—flat out. *What choice do I have?* she thought. *Without a boyfriend or future?*

Barely graduating from Dunnville High, Linda Klars enjoyed the worst grades ever, so her principal Mr. Sinclair said.

"You're your own man now," he went, fidgeting alongside a brand new electric guitar in his Toyota truck—and winking. "Endowed with utter failure!"

She smiled his smile.

It was July, 1976. With her parents' uneasy blessing, Linda was off to see the world. While her closest, more accomplished girlfriends went to Canadian universities. In the weeks leading to departure day, she listened to Abba and erased school.

The Swedish band choo-chooed through "Bang-A-Boomerang" and "Dancing Queen" as she stuffed blouses into a pink Sears suitcase and glanced warily at the List of Essentials mailed by the British Work-Stay Programme for Young Adults.

What happened? How could best friends deceive her like this? The frigging toadies studied, that's what—and sent out scads of applications. They were not, like naturally bright.

"Four months in England," she announced to everyone.

People smiled charitably for the dumbo of Dairy Side Road.

On a free afternoon in September at the Cornish river, Linda met Fabrizio Benedetti-Toc. He was reading *Yacht News* on the quayside—and smoked a black cigarette. In his billowy linen pants and green blazer, he seemed like a fish out of water. As much as she, in fact.

Linda waitressed—labour that would become her calling—at the Sir Humphry Davy in one of Cornwall's picturesque hamlets. Fringed by several cottages and a car park, the ivy-covered hotel, owned by Mr. and Mrs. Ambrose, stood quaintly on Helford riverbank. Between shifts, Linda was chambermaid, six days out of seven. No essays, no treacherous school friends, no barn chores. This was *real* graduation. She doused her loneliness in pints of shandy, and Walkers crisps, in a beer garden the size of a pasty pie.

At first, Linda thought the smoker was Middle Eastern. The goatee, his dark, liquid eyes. That late-twenties-hangdog air, the paunch. He resembled a sheikh, didn't he? In exile? Heavy jowls. A younger version of Mr. Sinclair, gone Aladdin.

The Arab pored over his news.

She smirked, remembering Dunnville's principal who considered students' oddities, except hers, as "talent in gestation." Into his forties, Mr. Sinclair sang with a band, Deadly Sores, at every prom. Their album "Grainy Spot" never quite gestated.

Linda watched late-summer hikers on the ferry at Helford Passage. Windswept faces, outward bound. En route to Falmouth from the Lizard peninsula, so she imagined, though never bothered to ask. She was too impressed for hard facts. England and the English were enchantment itself. The British Isles a Neverland. How awesome could awesome get?

"Big Ben's stopped," he said, startling her. "In London."

"Big Ben?"

She thought she knew what Big Ben was—but couldn't picture it.

"The great clock at Westminster," he said. "It's not ticking at present."

"Gee, no?"

"England's lost the time!"

Linda, her mousy hair tied back for work, chuckled. She couldn't see England getting lost for long. This cloudy island, the little she had witnessed of it, was a funky operation, if eccentric. People were resourceful, it seemed to Linda. They "mucked in" as Mrs. Ambrose would say, "despite themselves."

Fabrizio was everything Linda had not envisaged in a boyfriend. Older by a good decade. Tubby. A cement factory boss from Milan, he owned a vacation property on the hill. Invited her to visit.

She took the bait.

Is this romantic? Linda wondered. His clotted accent and linen pants did make her blush. Her stomach turned somersaults. Shouldn't romance be more subtle, though? Drawn out?

It felt so easy. His attentiveness, the waxen eyes. Her craving the man's company, and flabby stomach. His kindliness. She had never experienced such intimacy, wanting every last detail.

Linda threw herself on the Italian's mercy.

He taught her digits, tongue. A whispered vocabulary of lovemaking beyond her ken, urgent and precise.

Every Wednesday at 3:30 PM, flabby "Fabby" met his sweetheart at Helford Passage. They sipped tea, ate whortleberry scones, and climbed the valley to Die Möwe, his summer hideaway beyond Helford river. The German name meant "Seagull."

"No phone, no pool," he said. "No mail, no TV."

"That sucks."

"It's ideal, *cara.*"

One afternoon in October, her first ever October out of Canada, they lay by the fire. She pointed to a cluster of photos on the side table: a stylish young couple, three children, one a mere baby. Dunes, grasses he called "sweet flag."

"It was our holiday," he said. "In Denmark, last year."

"Your kids?" as if Linda had not realized. *What kind of game am I playing?* she thought.

Fabrizio nodded. "A seagull marched into every shot."

Linda strained to see.

"Near the broken fence," he said. "Another on the Hornbaek sands, and that pest on our umbrella."

"What are their names?" she asked.

"No names."

"No, silly," Linda said. "Your family."

He pecked her cheek. "Sylvie is my wife."

She noted the woman's sun-bleached eyebrows and that Fabby disliked seagulls. In his pictures.

"Emil, Paolo, and Adrian are our sons."

"Who's the baby, then?"

"That's Adrian," he said, reaching for a lighter.

"Where are they now?"

"In Berlin with their mother and grandparents." He offered

her a Sobranie. "Let's keep them that way."

"You're divorced?"

"No, Linda."

She nestled closer, wondering whether to leave. "We don't talk about it, Fabrizio?"

"There's no point."

"You're divorcing her?"

"You're the prize, my love," he said, squeezing her wrist. "Give us time."

Linda mulled "us" over and took a black cigarette. "So you christened the cottage 'Seagull.'"

"Sylvie and I decided on 'Die Möwe.'"

"Why not the English word?"

He drew hard on the Sobranie. "'Gull' was the name Sylvie wanted in English."

"'Gull,' simply?"

He tossed the lighter high. She grabbed at it.

"Sylvie takes stands," he said.

The catch felt warm in her palm.

Fabrizio bought Linda a Grundig transistor radio and a work of fiction by the local author Daphne du Maurier to keep her company after long, tiring days at the hotel.

Gifts from a lover.

The novel was romance, as far as Linda could gather. She never read books, unless Dunnville assigned one, and then she borrowed study guides. Farm girls have no time, Linda used to tell herself. Even with Abba in the background, there were chores.

The tale was quite dotty, as Mrs. Ambrose liked to say of anything more complex than the *Daily Mail* or her "Pub Grub" menu. It concerned a rich woman, Dona and her tempestuous affair with a French pirate named Jean. Bored buccaneer Jean happened to moor his galleon *La Mouette*, which (of course) meant "Seagull," in one of the hidden creeks off Helford river, not far from Dona's country estate.

Linda hoped Fabrizio did not fancy himself a pirate. She had grown up amongst cattle lowing and geese. Her sex life with F.B. was too advanced as it was.

Dona, so Linda read, disguised herself as a cabin boy to accompany Jean on his raid of the British vessel *Merry Fortune*.

That was it. Linda tossed the book aside. She was not playing cabin boy to pirate Fabby.

Was she not?

More realistically, did she want to become his partner? Wife? Mother to his children? The questions bared their teeth and she had no answers.

One blustery Wednesday in late October, she and Fabrizio trekked as far as Frenchman's Creek, its water the shade of gunmetal. An inlet with abandoned quay. Beneath swaggering oaks and beeches, the couple spread a blanket. Fabrizio poured lemonade into plastic cups. Linda delved into her "love apple" sandwich.

Fabrizio undid his pants and knelt down.

With beech leaves tumbling over the napkins, Fabrizio slithered into Linda as though she were pudding.

Would Daphne or Dona do this? wondered Linda, her head knocking against a thermos flask. Make out in the pages, finished or unfinished, of du Maurier's book, this minute squashed in Linda's anorak pocket, rolled to keep her bottom up?

Who needed a training manual for romance?

She was *living—Creek* or no Creek.

The breeze chilled Linda's thighs.

Throughout autumn in her maid's attic bedroom, overlooking dustbins in the hotel parking lot, she tuned quietly to BBC programmes on Fabrizio's Grundig radio. Mao Zedong had died in September, and nations descanted. Jimmy Carter won the U.S. presidential election.

On Fabby's advice, Linda sought out punk rock on Radio Luxembourg, an offshore pirate station with intermittent signal. Lives beyond Daphne du Maurier flooded in and out like tidewater. This was Fabby's "disunited kingdom." She fell asleep to jazz voices and feasted on Fabrizio Benedetti-Toc. The shipping forecast droned on. Greenwich time pips rumbled her spine and split apart her dreams.

On a day off, when Fabrizio was away in Plymouth, she rode the 504 bus to Fowey and cancelled her flight to Canada. With the bounty, she purchased earphones and an antenna from Barnum's Electrical Goods. Linda acquired an upper-arm seagull tattoo from Rat-a-tat-Tats on Lostwithiel Street.

In Helford, she raised the volume and a black aerial on her radio. Made beds like a hornet to The Clash and Siouxsie and the Banshees. She folded more blankets in an hour than you could shake a stick at. (Or something like that. Mrs. Ambrose again).

✥

In early November, as they made their Wednesday pilgrimage to Die Möwe, Fabrizio explained his journey from Italy to Romania, a decade before. How he had met his wife Sylvie in Viscri, near its medieval *Weisskirch.* How she studied botany. How she persuaded him to stay a year.

"Didn't you have a job?"

"In Milan, yes."

Linda gazed at him.

"This was Italy in the sixties," he said. "*Il boom.* Anything was possible. Italy faced revolution. Pasolini made slum films and attacked the church."

"No 'Work-Stay Programme' for you?"

"I was young," he replied. "I'm a spontaneous man, still."

Linda admired that. "You'd fallen in love with Sylvie?"

"We were seventeen years old," he said. "Who knows anything at that age?"

"I'm eighteen, Fabby."

"You're in a different era, sweetheart."

Linda was not so sure.

"The following year, August 1967, there was excitement amongst the villagers," Fabrizio said. "The British Prince of Wales was in Viscri."

"Prince Charles of England?"

"He was my age, more or less, and he worshipped the lost-world feel of the place."

Viscri sounded as dull as Dairy Side Road.

"The prince liked horses and carts and wild flowers?"

"He was starting at Cambridge University in the October," Fabrizio said.

"So it was a vacation?"

"Number sixty-three on Viscri's only road became his."

"He bought a house?"

"The man wanted Viscri for always, yes!"

Is Fabrizio getting at something? Linda thought. Did he want her, like the English prince in Fabby's Romanian village, to live in Helford permanently? How could she afford the rent?

Was this an Italian proposal?

Or did Fabby see *himself* as the visiting royal ... craving a bit of Linda forever? She could be his mistress. He was telling her a story-story, that was it. Like he did with his daft *Frenchman's Creek*. This was Fabby's way of getting serious.

"Sylvie was observing me drink too much *palinka* at the Viscri tavern," he said. "At that moment, his royal highness was on the slope. You could see a group of men in short-sleeves and chinos. They were seated on the grass."

Linda and Fabrizio reached the driveway to Die Möwe on the brow of Helford Hill. Yachts plied the river below.

"You talk too much," she said, abuzz with questions.

Fabrizio waved her aside. "'Prostrate yourself, pay your respects!' the innkeeper hollered at me. His name was Alexandru. 'In our traditional way!'"

"But you're Italian," Linda said. "You were a *tourist* in Romania."

"Alexandru egged people on," Fabrizio replied. "'Why would I prostrate myself?' I asked him. 'I'm no royalist.' 'No-one else has the guts,' he shouted back. 'Do it!' Sylvie cheered me along as always. 'I'm pissed!' I told them."

"Oh no."

"Alexandru saddled two mares and strong-armed me onto a

horse, and Sylvie onto another."

"You galloped into the sunset?"

"One of the prince's bodyguards shielded him," said Fabrizio. "Another man stood and pulled out a revolver."

Linda winced.

"We quickly reined in the horses and climbed off," he said. "We lay face down before Charles and his companions."

A lull.

"What happened?"

"The horses snorted, and the prince's friends made jokes about a Pied Piper leading children out of villages."

"That wasn't very nice."

"Sylvie and I got to our feet," he said. "In Italian, I delivered a welcome and the prince accepted. We were there twenty minutes or more, exchanging our impressions of Viscri and Romania. They offered us an Ursus beer."

"You're lucky the security didn't shoot you."

"'Fabrizio and I are going to marry,' Sylvie told Prince Charles, before we went to find our horses behind the clearing. It was the first I heard of such a thing. "'Fabrizio and I are going to marry," Sylvie?' I asked her back. 'We've no choice now,' she said. The Englishmen looked very bemused."

"You got married, anyway?"

Fabrizio lifted the latch of Die Möwe. "You don't pass up moments like that, Linda."

"Sylvie was pregnant?" She followed him into the hallway, kicked off her new wellington boots. "As well as drunk?"

"Neither."

He turned to embrace her.

"I don't understand, Fabby."

She leaned in close.

Fabrizio looked embarrassed. "Sylvie made up my mind, *cara*." He kissed Linda hard.

The following week, Fabrizio missed their Wednesday rendezvous.

It was 4:30 PM by the time Linda reached the top of the hill. Dusk in the valley.

She peeped through the hedgerow into Die Möwe. There was a Ferrari sports car with foreign license plates parked awkwardly in the driveway.

Linda stood at the gate.

On the terrace above Helford Passage, Fabrizio drew a woman to his side. He caressed her cheek.

Linda turned.

"Come and say hello to Sylvie." Fabrizio's voice sounded tight. He walked quickly around the car, followed by his wife.

"You must be the Canadian." Sylvie extended her hand.

Linda nodded. Beneath her feet, the gravel choked.

"My husband is returning to Berlin," Sylvie said. "Our boys need him."

Linda stared at Fabrizio who opened his hands as though giving up.

"Is everything okay?" Linda said. For an instant, she thought the children might be ill.

Sylvie smirked. "It's not."

"Awesome of you to drop by, Linda." He put on a strange, American accent.

"It is?" Linda felt confused.

Fabrizio shrugged.

"It's over," Sylvie told the Canadian.

As Linda tried to figure out whether Fabrizio's marriage had ended, Sylvie glanced impatiently at Helford Hill. "Perhaps next summer?" she said. "He does this like clockwork, you know. Was he reading *Yacht News*?"

"Will you return to Olde England ?" he asked, seemingly buoyed by his wife's sarcasm.

Sylvie slapped her husband's mouth.

Clutching his jaw, he strolled up to Linda.

She ran.

"It's not so bad," he said. "Really."

Sylvie tutted.

At first, Linda did not understand what she felt beyond humiliation and pain. European men had mistresses. What was it with Mr. and Mrs. Benedetti-Toc? Didn't they know? Linda could forgo marriage. *Mistress* was okay. Permanent mistress, that is. Not a summer spree.

The following Wednesday, determined to thrash things out, she made her way to Die Möwe.

From the road, Linda saw that every shutter was barred. Garden furniture, lanterns, cleared. At the gate, for once bolted, "No Entry."

Linda stood at a telegraph pole and sobbed. She pictured Fabby's green blazer and linen pants—of Day One. She realized he had never again worn them. Nor read *Yacht News*.

She cried some more. Until a post office van passed.

At the Sir Humphry Davy, she cranked the radio. Fabby had her address. He would contact her. No-one abandoned love like theirs. Was it love? Or just a spot of meaning in her life?

I'm so sick of questions, she thought. *I'm not sure what I feel. Maybe I never felt anything—other than loneliness.*

In December, the Sex Pistols let rip on "Today," Bill Grundy's television show. Many staid listeners were outraged. A BBC radio phone-in glutted itself with indignation. Johnny Rotten had said "shit," and Steve Jones called the presenter Mr. Grundy, who was drunk, a "dirty fucker." It sounded childish to Linda Klars but she felt the rockers' smouldering rage. Broadcasting was not half this fun in Canada.

No word from Fabby.

If he could dress up and stand on a quayside, so could she. In Fowey, Linda bought two pairs of black jeans, a t-shirt and used bomber jacket from Rashleigh Flats—along with a plane ticket home. She dolloped on crimson eyeshadow and fixed a safety-pin in her nostril.

Mr. and Mrs. Ambrose seemed delighted by the sea-change in their employee.

Linda left Canada as Abba. She returned Sex Pistol.

At the evening surgery of Dunnville Wellness Centre, Linda lay down on an examination table. Her tattooed arm aloft. Snow-flecked, red poinsettias jostled at the lakeside window. In Linda's earphones, Johnny Rotten's album "Never Mind the Bollocks" thundered around her skull.

"Breathe," said Dr. Frederic Di Tirro, middle-aged heart-throb to his staff, as he gunned laser light into the year-old Cornish seagull.

"Are you enjoying the music?" he asked.

She lifted the headset. Lyrics from "Holidays in the Sun" roared out.

Dr. Di Tirro, a sprig of holly and berries in his lapel, repeated his question more loudly and continued the erasure of a wing. To Linda it felt like hot grease spattering her skin. How many more weeks to remove a tattoo? This was her third excruciating visit and during the busy festive season at Dairy Side Diner.

"Enjoying myself."

"Are you?" he yelled. "To lessen the pain, is it, the music?"

The Sex Pistols struck up "God Save the Queen." Johnny Rotten and Sid Vicious tore the throat from a chorus.

"Yeah."

"Ah! That's what I thought you were doing."

She lip-synched her way into more "Bollocks" verse.

"I like seeing you," said Dr. Di Tirro, running the length of a scapular with his pistol. "Your mother's a patient of mine."

"Do you really?"

"When there's no future," screeched the voice in Linda's head. The laser crackled through a solitary feather. "How can there be sin?"

"Yeah," he said.

The laser pulsed on. Dr. Di Tirro shot several quill tips and a downy barb. "We'll go for a coffee afterwards, shall we?"

Linda pouted. She imagined billowy linen pants, a cigarette, horsemen in a prince's meadow. Dr. Di Tirro looked up from his one-winger.

"You dirty fucker," she said.

"Well, keep going, chief. Keep going," Dr. Di Tirro suggested. "Go on, you've got another ten seconds. Say something outrageous."

"Prick."

The second wing's covert—and alula—went up in smoke.

"Go on, again," he said. "It stops the stinging."

"Bastard."

Dr. Di Tirro nailed a last after-feather in a blaze of green and gold. "Your future dream," Johnny Rotten squawked, "is a shopping scheme."

"Two, one, zero," said Di Tirro, gunslinger to the marked and stained. "You survived."

She could not take any more hits.

Dr. Di Tirro studied the inflamed handiwork. "That's it for tonight." He brushed an icepack across her sore skin. "The wings are gone."

Linda eyeballed the splotchy spaces. "I've had enough."

She clambered to her feet.

"You can't keep the bird's torso, Linda," he said. "Book another appointment."

"Nah."

On her right upper arm, like a deadly penguin, the creature stood proud, sea-green and jaundiced, slammed into veiny poinsettias.

"How about that Christmas coffee?"

"I'll get the bird re-inked," she said, ignoring him. Linda buttoned-up her parka. "I've decided."

"Arms behind its back?"

She smiled merrily for the doctor. "You need to get out more, Dr. Di Tirro."

Gently closing his door.

Dog Stare

Dear Liz:

My, aren't we full of surprises, Liz McFadden? Not a dicky-bird out of you for ten years, and now this letter from Manaus, if you please. The CBC did a story on James's kidnapping for last night's news. There have been phone calls and there's a snippet inside the Toronto newspapers, too. Did you contact Reuters or something? Where did they get that dreadful mugshot of my son? A frosh party? I remember hearing a radio report, back in January, that he was missing. No doubt his hapless brother Alex and my former husband are glad for the additional publicity on their floundering gold mine. Judging by the stock-market price, it could do with a nudge. As for James. Poor James. But you needn't have written, dear.

You will know, or perhaps not, that since Nick and I divorced in 1990, I've had nothing to do with the boys or him. Appalling, isn't it? More of a mutual disregard really. I knew Alex had joined his father in Bom Intento but, to be honest, I thought

James was in Toronto with you, doing the odd bit of consulting anywhere but Brazil or near his brother and father. Poor James. As his mother I should show more concern, I know. You're likely shocked by my indifference, but the news of his disappearance leaves me cold. I'm sorry.

Eleven years ago our family, as I knew it, came to an end on that Isle of Skye. It wasn't completely your fault, as you later discovered, I trust. In fact, your conduct was the half of it. I never blamed you or was critical of your slip with that islander (I don't recall his name). But after my husband Nick's treatment of <u>me</u>, after I defended your actions, I gave up on him. When my son Alex backed Nick up, I dropped him too. Your husband vowed never again to speak to Nick or Alex after the way they treated me. I was proud of James for that. Standing up to his self-righteous, complicit brother and their brutal old man whom I'd so mistakenly married. Your affair drew more than a little attention to everything wrong in my own life.

To my chagrin, however, James eventually included me in the fatwa and closed the door on his mother, father, and brother. Figure that one out. Maybe he's mellowed vis à vis his brother and father. Certainly, and oh how typical, I am still demonized. Boys and their mothers! These days I've little time or patience for the McFaddens, to tell you the truth. I've reverted to my maiden name: Chartler. Best decision of my life. Maybe James is missing, maybe he's dead. I hope not. But where Nick, Alex, and he are concerned, believe nothing that you haven't witnessed first hand. They're a barbaric clan, and James never comes out on top.

You ask for advice, not family recriminations. But, at the risk of sounding blunt or insensitive (given that your own parents are deceased and you are an only child), a mother-in-law's counsel might serve you well, but I do not wish to get involved with your predicament. I hold no grudges, Lizbie, but cannot surely be expected, after so much time, to demonstrate any stalwart, familial concern just because it now suits you to break a silence.

I'm in the process of moving to England to see my days out there. This Toronto house and its unwieldy English garden are in tremendous flux, which I'm attempting to master. As I write, I'm surrounded by packing cases. Outside on the terrace there is every manner of gardening tool, not to mention garbage bags and new plants, shrubs ready for the ground. I'm awash in chores.

If you do your sums, Liz, you'll know that I'm now seventy-six years old and a little shaky on my pins. My picturesque garden, as far as Canadian weather allows, preoccupies me day and night, especially as I try to get its flowerbeds and wilder part beyond the greenhouses under control before I relinquish it to the new owners. I've become witheringly selfish, I suppose, living solo with my books, booze, cigarettes, and herbaceous catalogues. What else could a woman wish for? Into the bargain, and like some island I guess, I'm taking myself off to another island. Pandora's Box in reverse, if you will. Closing up shop. That terrible privilege of the superannuated. How you and your generation must resent me.

Having said that, for the purposes of this letter I will offer you some pearlies to brood upon, for what they're worth. But please

Liz, do not even countenance the idea of further dialogue. I'm too jaded for it. Many regrets, but I intend to savour my going out to pasture without any interference from the McFaddens or from you. To abort our late, illustrious Marshall McLuhan, in my case neither the medium nor its message are of any consequence. No letters from you please, no phone calls, e-mails. Nothing. I insist. Solitude must be absolute. I have earned every second of it.

… You ask how to proceed in Manaus. You're in the Brazilian city of short-lived splendour, my girl. Its opulent architecture and the mansions, as you're aware by now, are the result of a rubber boom in the 1890s. Take its message to heart. Nick, Alex and your husband are consumed by the prospect of smash-and-grab riches (though they occasionally go to great pains to conceal it). They seek and will find, but then will have to find over and over. Their appetites are without satiation or human regard. Take conscience of your adopted city. It's telling you something.

Six months you've resided there, you tell me. Many might think that whatever means you're using to survive are means enough. But yes, just as that Englishman Sir Henry Wickham's pilfering of Amazon rubber seeds and planting them in Malaya destroyed Manaus's fortunes, so of course nothing lasts. You're right to feel solitary, particularly as you try to locate my son James. Solitude is a friend, Liz. Even though its "splendour" is hard to stomach now and then. Don't run away from it, or from what it offers.

Might I suggest that in your grief and frustration you do some honest, hard work? As you might know, I've developed a modest reputation as a landscape watercolourist. My sustenance, between the painting, is a German poet: Rilke. Are you familiar with his work? Probably not. Rainer Maria Rilke? He can be oh-so-delicate at times, but I must say he's helped me a great deal. His letters on Cézanne and to a young poet, I often dip into. You might do the same. I know you trained at the Upper Canada School of Art when James was in mining at the University of Toronto. What happened? I never did catch on. Surely you didn't spend year after year drawing so that one day you could enslave yourself in the institution's administrative offices?

For the decade or so I knew you, your main preoccupation, apart from very public fretting about your daughter Heather's schooling, was how you looked and whether you could make it to our cottage at weekends. In fact, your life seemed abuzz with frantic dashing about from one rather meaningless activity to another, whether James was in town or not. <u>YOU WERE TERRIFIED OF PAINTING.</u> Never, never did a sketch emerge from those expensively manicured fingers of yours; and what about that creative tension expended on shoes?! The days of young ladies learning the arts for mere accomplishment went out with Jane Austen, you know. I advise you to <u>draw</u>. At least until there's something more definitive about your husband's whereabouts. Get yourself paper, charcoal, paints. Brush or pencil, you know what to use. Install yourself in that wretched jungle and take the place up. Snap-snap!

To lean on my poet, I suspect you're feeling something akin to Cézanne, who in Aix-en-Provence would return home after a day's hard graft at Mont Sainte-Victoire bubbling over with troubles and misgivings. Much like you after a day's grappling with that rockface of James's disappearance, I wouldn't wonder. In time, Cézanne realized how these powerful feelings depleted him. You too spoke of enervation from the hopelessness you feel in tracing James. Cézanne worried about everything as well, Liz: colour, the state of the planet, his work, industrialization. How does Rilke put it? Here it is, "Out there, something vaguely terrible on the increase." You must feel this too. Horrified at what might come to be? What the "vaguely terrible" will expose? I think so. Go paint your Mont Sainte-Victoire, my child. Let it engage you. Be crazed with it.

You bemoan solitude like someone who can't believe her luck. I shudder at your phony misery. Besides, to judge from what you tell me, have you ever not been alone, especially in recent years? Maybe this is the first time you've looked solitude, real solitude, in the face. My poet would tell you to love it and embrace the suffering it causes you. That does sound a trifle "S and M" doesn't it? Or, Protestant masochism. There's truth to it, though. Just remember it's inner solitude we're talking about, and that needs your attention. You'll find some true solace there, not to mention confidence. Excuse the New Age tone! Patience and calm are the ticket, dear.

Remember, too, in this recent exploring, that your daughter Heather is in Manaus as well. No short-lived splendour is Heather. Don't neglect her, Liz. Two solitudes do not a mother and child make, believe me. Be mindful of your daughter. Don't follow my example with the McFaddens and think only of yourself.

Once in England, settled in so very cute a Norfolk cottage, I shall look forward to hearing that your Brazilian paintings are on display in the gallery your institute runs (and which rejected my own work some years ago). I'm certain that, with application, yours will fare better.

Get a good night's rest, rise early, and take a boat (without the guide) to Janauari Ecological Park. I went there myself several times between visits to that godforsaken mine in Bom Intento. You'll find your subject: a plant, flower, an obliging three-toed sloth. I envy you the trek. I do. Don't be frightened by any of it, nor by that creeping ribbon of solitude. Face it. Paint what you see. <u>Dog stare.</u>

Meanwhile, back to a wheelbarrow anxiously awaiting me beneath the maple trees. Such overgrown paths to clear! Then later, more packing of china. Be safe, young Liz. Let's keep our fingers crossed about James.

Kind regards,
Catherine Chartler

P.S. I suggest that you leave Hotel Manaus and find an inexpensive room, say near the Centro Cultural Palácio Rio Negro. I enclose the address of a Brazilian woman, Alma Olinto, whom I met on one of my three visits to Manaus in 1989-90 (the divorce). In fact, I'll write her a note this morning, to introduce you. She used to run a collective near the Museu do Homen do Norte on Avenida 7 de Setembro. They make meticulous coloured lanterns, floral shoppers, photo frames, and boxes out of jute. A generous, worldly lady, part-Tikuna Indian, who'll offer you wisdom. She doesn't have much time for first-world women down on their luck, I warn you. So don't do too much whining. She's got the keys to that city of short-lived fortune and will show you the right doors. <u>Use that woman.</u> <u>Not me.</u> You're on the verge of something tremendous, I sense that deeply. Leave Catherine the geriatric out of it, I beg you. She has a garden to tame. Solitude is the greatest gift, my dear. Take it.

Catherine

An Island in the South Pacific

"A shilling and twopence to Birmingham New Street is nothing, you know," Violet said as they hurried along the platform through a group of soldiers and families lining up at Walsall town station.

In borrowed stiletto heels, the two young women had run from Froggatt's factory—"Leather Goods to the Empire and Commonwealth"—to the ticket window. Ladies hurrying on a muggy Saturday afternoon. 1954. August Bank Holiday weekend.

Seven days left of foster-parentlessness for Nancy. While Edwin and Mabel Proffit basked in the Blackpool sun.

"We should shop in the smoke more often," Nancy said. She raised her voice, playing Violet's game. They stepped toward the rear of the one-o'clock train. "There's an hour before the show starts."

In our ever-so-full and glamorous lives.

Nancy smelled Froggatt's Leather and Dye beneath her friend's Eau de Chantilly Rose as they sat themselves inside a compartment rapidly filling with people.

"Shame Peter Threnody's not coming," said Violet. She looked about.

"I don't think so," replied Nancy. "Would you have him?"

"At your age, I wouldn't have anyone." Violet opened a Boots compact and scrutinized her face.

"Starting later with men, you are, Vi."

We never escape the factory, thought Nancy. Her best friend dabbed powder.

The scent of forget-me-nots.

"Eighteen's hardly late, Nancy Smith. Don't be blaberen."

"Fifteen's not so young, neither."

Nancy gazed at posters and a group of Teddy Boys. *It's marrow in the bone this leather pong*, she thought. *Everything you do is Froggatt's doing. But not this weekend.*

"Why don't you invite Peter to meet your minder?" asked Vi.

"Are you coddin? Meet Albert Mallinder?"

"Why not?"

"Uncle Albert doesn't want blokes near me. He's like Mabel and Edwin about 'em."

"Peter's a different can o' beans," said Violet. "Can't you tell?"

"*You* take Peter Threnody, Vi, and I'll take a holiday like my foster parents."

"He's steady, love. You don't make fun of a steady young fella these days. Few and far between."

"Everyone loves him. It's boring."

"Keen more like, Nancy. What's the matter wi' you? Peters of this world bring home the bacon."

"An' a coffin."

"He lives in those new flats along Venus Close."

"I'm not courtin' a flat, Vi."

Violet took out Max Factor lipstick and some tissue paper.

"Who do you go walking with, Vi? Up Memorial Gardens of a Sunday?"

"Someone like our gaffer, Mr. Woods'd do me fine, thank you very much."

"He's a right wag mon."

"Don't get his hands dirty, has some class."

Nancy pictured Mabel and Edwin's hasty departure for Blackpool. This very day last week. Would she ever want to go for a summer holiday with Peter Threnody?

"Your Peter's a gentleman compared to some. Wouldn't see him traipsin' up an' down Lucy Street of a Saturday night."

"Y'would, too."

"Up the Monkey Run? Peter Threnody?" said Violet.

"Where d'you think I met him, Vi? Holy Joe's tea-party?"

"You go up the Bridge of a Saturday night?"

"Like a dog at a fair, Vi."

"Nancy! At your age! As far as the Royal Oak?"

"You know it?"

"You're uncouth," Violet said.

Did Edwin and Mabel go a-courtin'-o? The Proffits now getting their money's worth, as Edwin Proffit saw it—four pounds ten a week, full board—over hushed breakfasts and dinners; deck chairs and cups of tea on the pier, before a night tut-tutting along the front—"Too many Spivs and Creepers, for my likin'"—and in the pubs. Edwin always argued with Mabel about the holiday—once they had made it back to Walsall with their shells and sticks of rock.

Nancy smirked.

"Are you havin' me on, Nance?"

They both erupted in giggles.

"I'd be *frit!* I met Peter at the corner store, y'saft bat."

"You had me worried, wench."

"Bought me a sherbet dab, he did."

A postcard of Blackpool's autumn "Illuminations" had arrived yesterday. Wednesday last, a picture of the Cliffview Terrace Guesthouse: Mabel Proffit had forgotten to pack her posh Firefly stockings, and summer skirt (so she thought); the food was changeable, weather cooperative; was Nancy being a good girl for Uncle Albert Mallinder? Edwin and Mabel hoped she was enjoying the stitching at Froggatt's and was going to bed early to be fresh for the next morning. Did they bury Mrs. Caddlestone? Love, Mum and Dad.

Who gave a tinker's damn? Is this what she and Peter would do as grown-ups? Nancy could not take her eyes off a poster, next to the British Rail Parcels office: "Whole World for the Asking," it read. "Immigrate to Australia."

"Tell you what, Nance."

"What, Vi?"

"Find me the perfect bloke and I'll do the same for you."

How Nancy wished she were going further than Birmingham. Further than Peter Threnody. Maybe she'd follow the Froggatt's leather goods overseas. Pack herself in with some saddles, razor straps, dog collars, and a few footballs.

"I'll be waitin' forever, knowing you, Vi."

"What do you mean?"

"Three years is it you've been lookin'?"

"Now is that fair, Nance? I'm just particular."

"There's another word for it, Vi."

"Is there?"

"Maybe you do need my help."

"You're a babby, Nancy Smith."

Blackpool, Nancy wondered. *Would I miss it?*

No. She would not miss it. In fact, maybe it would disappear somehow. It normally did until December 25th when, in two days of holiday nostalgia and a few bottles of Ansells Nut Brown ale, Edwin and Mabel Proffit would discuss returning. But to a different boarding-house where the owners were not so stuffy. Edwin was against stuffy. So they would change accommodation, if not the destination.

When Easter came around, the Cliffview Terrace did not seem as bad as that—"Better the devil you know," he would half-say, every year around Easter Sunday. The Resurrection got him worked up. That, daffodils, calves, Nut Brown, and the rabbits on greeting cards.

So Edwin forgave *stuffy.* Mabel bought a few more floral dresses. They booked the industrial fortnight: Cliffview Terrace.

"How many men have you chucked, then?"

"I watch 'em at Froggatt's and along Kendrick Road, Vi."

"You get savvy from watchin'?"

A married couple—twenties—seated themselves opposite Nancy and Violet.

"Why not?" said Nancy. "I wouldn't expect anything from blokes in person."

"Not round our way, any road," whispered Violet.

"Not round anywhere, Vi."

"Why's that then?"

"'Cos I can do it meself. That's why."

"All, Nancy?"

"Well not *that*."

Violet fanned at her mouth to stop tittering. "I'd like to see you try, Nancy."

"Five years, Vi?"

"Then you'll be twenty."

"Five years to get meself independent, and a man where I want him?"

"That's it."

"If I lose?"

"You'll be like the rest of us, Nance."

The steam-engine began.

"What's that then, Vi?"

"Gasbaggin', love," said Violet. She raised her voice. "Keepin' to our own end."

"I see." Nancy spoke quietly. "Where does that put you?"

"I'll name me choices in a little while," replied Violet. She lowered her voice. "I'm content enough."

"Bet's on then, Vi. Just you watch me."

Violet smiled toward the people across. "Everyone starts to calm down after a while."

"Give up, you mean, Vi?"

"I mean we get realistic."

"That so?"

"It is."

"What happened to 'It's wha' y'can gerraway with'?"

"Christ, you're prying, Miss Smith."

Nancy's eyes followed a cheerful advertisement as the train slipped away from the last of the station. She had thought, at first, it was concerned with dental paste: a beaming, clean-cut man in an open shirt, and sports jacket. A toothy, girly wife and a pair of babies, beaming too—or screaming—under the sunniest of skies. A massive white and yellow steamship behind them. Postbox-red funnels. "Brush your teeth or miss the boat?" No, there were passports, tickets, and Australian dollars in the father's perfect-looking hands. This was serious: how to leave England and be glad about it.

"It's overcrowded here," said Violet, catching Nancy's line of vision.

"Eh?" Nancy gaped at the poster-man's wife as she shrank away. The woman wore a sky-blue polkadot skirt, same style as Mabel's for Blackpool, that curled like arms around the smiling, or grimacing, infants.

"Winston Churchill's trying to get rid of us," said Violet, her voice loud again.

Nancy wished her best friend would stop this: broadcast on, broadcast off. "Don't be an ape, Vi."

Is it that much fun? thought Nancy. *Immigrating.* She considered those teeth. That awful skirt with spots on it.

"He is, too," Violet said. "Assisted passages."

"Isn't it an opportunity?" Nancy asked. *Or am I on Edwin Proffit's side?* she wondered. Too many potholes in life, as well as in a dress. The holiday morning on the landing, Mabel did look like a sieve, and so did that Mrs. Going-To-Australia-Thank-God. Too many dots to stumble over, riddlin' the gleeds. *I'd look like a sieve too. That's the message: Nancy, it's saying, stay put in England—at least until you've got the wardrobe, if not the teeth.*

Nancy looked—as best she could—at her own get-up, then crossed her legs: Mabel's white lacquer sheen, pleated nylon skirt;

Mabel's lime-green-and-cream striped blouse; the flesh-tone Fire-fly stockings.

"Opportunity, Nance?" said Violet. "They can't transport us for nickin' a loaf o' bread no more."

"Give over."

Violet glanced opposite. The man appeared to nod.

"So they're paying the boat fare instead," Vi added.

Maybe I am dressed for the immigration bit, thought Nancy: Mabel's pink cardigan, the white handbag and shoes. *Just the gear for an ocean liner. Thank you, Mabel Proffit.*

"Why not immigrate, Vi?"

"Australia's just the place for the likes of you and me, Nance. La-di-dah-di-dah."

"Yellow belly."

"Nowt wrong wi' Walsall," said the man opposite.

"That's right, ain't it, Nance?"

"No, Vi."

"What's wrong wi' Walsall, then?" said the man.

"Nothin'" replied Nancy. "If yower a piece o' leather."

The couple smiled politely.

"Things happen to cows and bulls around here," Nancy said. *Why not travel to Birmingham every week?* she thought. *To see this matinee and that at the Theatre Royal?* She felt so posh she scared herself.

"Australia's not the answer," said the man. His eyes blinked rapidly.

"Why not?" replied Nancy.

"Your Peter Threnody's uncle and aunt immigrated to Sydney," said Violet. "Three months later, they're back in Walsall."

"'omesick?" the man's wife asked. She held a carrier bag in her lap and a folding umbrella.

Three Teddy Boys and a girl stood at a blustery level-crossing.

"What would y'expect?" said Violet.

"We're not accustomed to Aussie ways," replied the man.

"You've thought about it, then?" said Nancy.

"Wha'?"

"You've thought about movin' t'Australia?"

"Oh, ah."

"Who 'asn't?" said the man's wife.

"What with the missus, you know," he said.

The missus nodded.

"Littl'uns?" Violet asked.

"Nay," said the man, pulling a face.

His wife toyed with the pleats of her umbrella.

"Couldn't stand it out there, eh?" said Violet.

"Too many foreigners," replied the wife. She wrinkled her nose.

"There's plenty enough Pakis around *here*," said the husband. He checked the compartment.

"'e's right, y'know," said his wife.

"No better off than you'd be in Walsall?" Violet asked.

Nancy wondered how they would know.

"Put down roots, don't you?" said the man. "Wife. Job. Yower mates."

"Family, like," his wife agreed. She folded the pleats more tightly.

"He's not *my* Peter Threnody," whispered Nancy. She had heard enough from The Matrimony opposite.

"Eh, love?" said Violet. She looked uncomfortable.

"Peter and me aren't courtin'."

"Why aren't you?"

"'cos I wouldn't go all the way, Vi."

"Nancy!"

"I wouldn't."

"I should hope not."

"So it's over."

Violet shook her head.

"Plenty of fish in the sea," said Nancy. She winked in the direction of The Matrimony—who seemed drawn to the passing yards, cobbled streets, back-to-backs, and Victorian warehouses that bordered the railway line.

"Dead loss, you," said Violet. "'onestly!"

"Though I do like to feel him," Nancy explained, broadcasting on.

By the time the train reached Wednesbury Road and Willows Lane, a hush separated the four riders.

"Off to see your boyfriends?" said the man.

Nancy studied the empty carrier bag.

"Mind yer own business, Patrick," his wife told him.

"No," said Violet.

"Yes," said Nancy, at the same time.

Violet giggled. Her face turned the colour of a steamship funnel.

"Not sure, girls?" said the man.

His wife, too, seemed amused by their confusion. "Life's like that, ain't it?" she said. She dug a *South Staffordshire Chronicle* out of her carrier bag and handed it to Patrick.

"We're going to see who we can pick up," said Nancy. She looked his wife in the eye.

"*South Pacific*" said Violet. She glanced at Nancy. "It's a musical."

"What's that about, then?" asked Patrick. He pushed the newspaper away.

"We don't know," said Violet. "Do we, Nance?"

"Yes we do, Vi."

"Do we?"

"Come along, girls," Patrick said. "Stop yer ivverin' an' ovverin' an' get on wi'it." He seemed short of breath.

Nancy watched him. "Love and war," she said. There had been a notice in the *Walsall Observer* at the paper shop.

"On an island in the South Pacific," Violet added.

"We don't go in for that kind of thing," said the missus. She wrinkled her nose again.

"War or love?" Nancy asked.

No-one spoke. The missus laughed nervously.

"Musicals," said Patrick. He took the *Chronicle* from his wife's knee.

"No?" from Violet.

Nancy tried *toothy* like Mrs. Australia. "Neither do we," she said.

Blanks

zachary-hollinger@freewebnet.kingston.on.ca

JULY 4, CROOKED HOLLOW

Hi Zack, wherever you are. I landed that summer wage-slave job, labouring for Mrs. Dowling. She talks like the Queen of England and doesn't move her lips. When I got to her place, first day, to build the fishpond she wants, she'd already dug a huge fuckin' pit. She was standing next to it panting. Then she pointed to a stack of marble and introduced it to me as though each slab was a person: "El Roco de Alicante," "Blanco Macel y Traventina de Almeria," "Marron de Albacete."

45

I bowed my head like an idiot. Then she presented me, "Mr. Scott Haring."

"Hi," I said, to everyone.

"*Cerveza?*" she asked me. "Beer?" It was eight-thirty on a Monday morning! Very weird. So I think we'll get on fine. Everyone calls her "Jacky" for some reason. Maybe I'll have more luck being friends with rubble, one-on-one, and an old British biddy. You were certainly no-one to trust after I dropped out of college. I love sitting outside by Mrs. Dowling's pond. It helps.

Scott

P.S. I've worked out a strategy for the graduation ceremony in Kingston.

SH

Rose Haring was on time. Monday was bingo at the community centre—and she was the caller.

"I'm just mowing grass for Mrs. Dowling," Scott told his mother. "I've got expenses with the website I'm running."

Doug, Rose's husband, walked her to the front door.

"Mrs. Dowling's British like you, dear," he said.

"The worst kind," replied Rose. She tossed Scott *The Crooked Hollow Expositor.* "*You* get hunting for proper work, son. That woman will lead you astray."

"You'll miss the bus," said Doug. He checked his watch.

"Mrs. Dowling's like something out of Gilbert and Sullivan."

Rose fastened her purse. "She's ridiculous."

"Bye, Ma," said Scott, glancing at the Classifieds.

"Ignore your mum," said Doug. He watched his wife on Quarry Falls Road. "It's one of those British *class* things."

"Mrs. Dowling's no snob, Dad."

"It's the accent that puts people off," he told his son. "You go ahead and garden for her."

"Okay."

"Your mother worries about discipline, that's all. She thinks you daydream too much."

"I'll go garden."

"Just keep away from Mrs. Dowling's booze," said Doug looking for his TV remote. "And her gentlemen friends."

zachary-hollinger@freewebnet.kingston.on.ca
JULY 25, CROOKED HOLLOW

Hi Zack.

Wow, is this Mrs. Dowling … Jacky … up your alley. It's a real shame you didn't meet someone like her at Royal Military College instead of our officers and that jerk in C unit. She's so broadminded, and crazy about guys like you. I had to disappoint her by mentioning I'm into women and that I'm making big bucks from my Mantrap site.

"So why are you gardening?" she asked. I told her I was trying to please my nineteenth-century parents while I live with them. It's the truth.

"I don't want the folks to know how much money I'm making and on what." She thought that was hilarious and wants shares in my company!!! Jacky's men friends are cool too, by the way. If you'd met dudes like this instead of your trash-cruising on my Mantrap site, maybe you'd still be here.

It's a pity Jacky treats her gay-boys like servants, though. She's always asking them to run errands and drive her places. One guy does her laundry! They answer her phone when they're visiting. She does feed them occasionally, I guess. But they end up finishing the cooking because she gets into the gin.

I'm not doing much gardening. And, hey, she's already invited me to her villa in southern Spain (where that marble came from). You know, Zack, I'm going to go there to see the kind of life you missed out on. I want to feel how truly fucking wrong you were to top yourself. How about that for an on-your-knees confessional?

Scott

Get real, Mantrap guys. Be clear and specific about what you want. If you're looking for friendship, say so. Don't go talking to the guy who wants a three-way with poppers and videos. Be honest about your appearance and age. Forget ideal weights and sizes: average dick length is four to seven inches. If all you hear from the greetings is thirty men with eight-inch cocks, draw your own conclusions. We know about men who drive big cars.

zachary-hollinger@freewebnet.kingston.on.ca

Hi Zack.

Whenever I ask Jacky Dowling's age, she replies, "Late twenties, darling. You never ask a lady." She's at least seventy. "I adore young people," she says, over and over, in her theatrical way. "You live life uncensored." She's entertaining, I guess, like you were but it's sad at the same time. I've told her about RMC: how I dropped out in the final year, and how a few months later, you walked off Wolfe Island and never came back.

She's going to help me with a fake graduation diploma, to fool my parents, before I travel to Spain. Can you believe it?

You and I were going to see the world together through the forces, Zack. I'm keeping my part of the bargain. The travel part, anyway. I guess I flunked the discipline you and I both seemed to need. What a great summer it's turning out to be. I thought I'd be cutting grass.

Your amigo,
Scott

Scott, in rented "Scarlets-1M summer" dress uniform, waited on the campus of Royal Military College, Kingston. Barely visible from Precision Drive or from Billy Bishop Road, he stood beneath a couple of maple trees. A car honked. The folks were right on schedule: four hours late. He peered through the window. Jacky Dowling at the wheel.

His mother, in the back, looked upset.

"It's my fault," said Jacky, in her neatly ironed shirt. "The wretched Rover gave out in Oshawa."

"In the middle of nowhere." Doug raised his arms in despair.

"I'm so terribly, terribly sorry," said Jacky.

"No sweat," Scott told them.

"The car seized, son." Doug pointed to Jacky. "No oil in it."

Scott climbed in and hugged his mother.

Rose wiped her eyes.

He opened the convocation program and offered it to her.

"My name's at the top, look." Scott pressed his finger, heavily. "Haring."

"We're very proud," said Jacky.

"Let's go eat," Scott replied. He closed the program and shook it impatiently. "You must be starving."

zachary-hollinger@freewebnet.kingston.on.ca
SEPTEMBER 12, CROOKED HOLLOW

Well Zack, I'm in deep shit over the graduation. Jacky doctored a half-dozen convocation programs, like we planned. The night before the ceremony she showed me her back-room handiwork. She'd put my name AND YOURS on them! Just like they were in class: Haring, Hollinger! She refused to get them re-done because "it'd take too long." I prayed my parents wouldn't catch it. I should have done the printing myself. Jacky wore one of her men's white shirts to Kingston, by the way. I've told you how she often wears them. I can't quite see why. You'd have thought she'd try something fancier, especially for a hoax graduation. Ma was upset by the car breakdown, of course. What did I expect?

Later,
Scott

To stop a caller from contacting you, and to avoid hearing his greeting, press eight. Remember: there's always the power of pressing eight.

"Is Mrs. Dowling a dyke, Dad?"

"I don't know," said Doug. "British women often end up like that. They aren't anything really."

"Really."

"She's probably 'mummy' to those men she sees," Doug said.

Jacky sipped a fourth glass of champagne in the courtyard of Chez Piggy restaurant in Kingston.

"The war was very good to me, Doug. For a while, I was posted to a bomber station in southern England. Full of Canadians. Oh, those beautiful young men from Saskatchewan farms, and Alberta. Prime, and so fit ..."

She gazed at the limestone walls.

Aw, come on. You can do better than that. You have thirty seconds to record your greeting. Don't leave it blank. Tell other callers something

about you. A line of blanks may appear interesting to some. We know there's more to you than a silence. Please record your greeting now. Then press star.

"Those Canadian bomber crews, so far from home," Jacky went on. "My job was to take calls from Whitehall about the night's mission. In code, of course. Top secret, very important. Then off the boys would go. One evening I'd be drinking and dancing with them in the mess. Then, next time, a few faces missing."

"You must have had your favourites," said Doug.

Jacky was not listening. "Then more and more disappeared. Sometimes I wished I'd get the routings muddled, and the poor darlings would be saved."

"You started to dread the calls, I bet?" asked Rose.

"Silly of me, isn't it?" replied Jacky. "I like to think they parachuted to safety, missed the bullets and trees, and floated away from harm."

Rose pouted. "If only, huh?"

"Did you travel much, Jacky?" asked Doug. He refilled their glasses and toasted his son again.

"The high command discovered I was good at the diplomatic stuff," she said. "So I went chatting to top brass in our European capitals. Getting people to see eye to eye. Bloody exhausting."

More champagne arrived.

"Allow me, Rose," said Jacky. She uncorked the bottle as though swatting a fly.

BEEP

Raunchy fuck-pig master. Top. Looking for a bottom. Anything goes. My place. Downtown. No Bullshit. Want it rough? Call right now.

BEEP

Twenty-two-year-old cum-hungry college jock. Bubble butt. Swimmer's build. Five-eleven. A hundred and sixty pounds. Blue eyes. Clean-shaven. Brush-cut. Eight inches, shaved balls. Your place. Hot suck and fuck action. Like to service.

BEEP

You have reached the end of the greetings. To return to the main menu, press three. To re-record your greeting, press one.

"Don't you find Crooked Hollow quiet?" said Doug.

"I have my hands full," Jacky replied. "Friends, my place in Spain."

"New faces, like Scott," said Doug.

"Of course! My rock pool!" Jacky patted the boy's arm. "Besides, the paintings and antiques I inherited from my family are at the Hamilton university gallery now."

"That's nice," said Rose. "You followed them here?"

"From Montreal," Jacky replied. "I worked for Air Canada, for decades."

"You must be glad to get away from cities and airports," said Doug.

"Crooked Hollow is as near to a country home as I will ever get again, after England," Jacky told them.

"You don't want to return to the U.K.?" said Rose.

"Too many memories," replied Jacky.

"I feel the same way about the old country," Rose said.

"Is that so?" said Jacky. She smiled and reached for the bread basket. "I would never have guessed."

BEEP

In my car. Don Valley Parkway. Looking for a blow-job in the East End. Shoot me a message.

BEEP

BEEP

Hi. My name's Stephen. I'm nineteen years of age and I'm not into baths or bars. I'm looking to talk and make friends with someone my own age in the Kingston area. Long term.

BEEP

Hot guy. Skinhead type. Tattoos, goatee. Thirty-five, eight-inch rock-hard cock. Scouting for a boy over twenty. Cops in uniform a plus. Wanna plough a creamy tight hole. No fems. Or fats. Buzz me.

BEEP

Another guy has sent you a message. Here it is:

"'Zachary Hollinger'?" said Rose. She studied the convocation program, smoothing it on Chez Piggy's checkered tablecloth. "What is his name doing here?"

Scott reached for the page. "It must be someone else."

"Zachary?" Doug asked. He rubbed at his spectacles. "Scott's friend?"

"It's his day, too, I believe," said Jacky.

Scott blushed.

Doug cleared his throat.

"Scott can't have mentioned it, Jacky," said Rose. The name "Jacky" seemed to stick to the roof of her mouth. "It's not something he'll talk about."

"Zachary passed on," Doug said. He squirmed in his place. "Two years ago."

"Tragically," Rose added.

"I'm here, remember," said Scott.

The convocation program lay open on the table. Rose rested her fingers upon it.

"Yes," Jacky said. "They loved one another."

Scott stared at the blur of scarlet font. "I never said *that*." Tears welled in his eyes.

Jacky—ears ever on Whitehall—sat before the Harings. "It could be honorary."

"Did you *alter* this list of graduates?" Rose asked her.

"What?"

"Did you 'fix' this convocation program, Mrs. Dowling?"

"It's my fault," said Scott. He wiped his mouth.

Rose stood. "How foolish do you think we are?"

"It was Scott's day," said Jacky. "I did what I could for both of them."

"Spare me the heroics," Rose snapped. She looked from Jacky to her son and back. "We're leaving, Doug."

"Come along, Scott." He reached for his son's arm. "You can't interfere in people's lives like this, Mrs. Dowling."

"Do you have any idea?" Rose asked. "What it's like to live, *for two years*, with a grieving son?"

"I will drive you," said Jacky.

"We'll get the train," Rose replied. "You've driven enough."

zachary-hollinger@freewebnet.kingston.on.ca
SEPTEMBER 14, CROOKED HOLLOW

Hey Zack.

I'm still at Quarry Falls Road. But house-sitting for Jacky. She's Spain-side for nine months. I finished her pond. It's an odd, kooky shape, like that whale's eye we saw on Grand Manan. Remember that? The Antichrist look! The fucker leaks too. Her fish are on code red.

The graduation was a bugger's muddle. Like a twat, I never confronted Jacky about why doctoring a few convocation programs took so long. She had the originals a week.

Sometimes, Jacky Dowling's giddy, man. Or just plain willful. She spends the time on her deck, in those shirts, staring at tops of fir trees, pissed on gin. Looking for parachutes or personal columns, or whatever. Ma and Pa noticed your name, under mine, on the program, of course. This week we've had talks to end talking. It'll take months to get over it. The old man calls Jacky "Rigger Mortis." Ma wanted to sue.

We're into an Indian summer right now. I grab the cellphone, and a beer, and sit out back under the trees (Jacky-style, by her panicking carp!!) listening to the chatline. Loony, huh? Fireflies mill around. I wait for those blanks, you know—they fuck everyone up. Those callers who don't speak.

Scott

Seriously

"I'm from Count Dracula's neck of the woods," he told us at the furniture show where we first met. I guess he tickles our fancy. The exotic Transylvanian.

My wife Linda and I have known Emil Toc for ten years. At one stage, he lived in our house for six months during a lay-off from work. He had no money.

Today's visit—in this chill no-man's land between Boxing Day and New Year—is a dicey prospect. To be sure he is an original. Look where he comes from. His family lives somewhere south or east of Cluj-Napoca, Romania. A village named Viscri.

Emil is very different from our other friends. More *considered* about everything, some would say. Slow. We do not put him and them together. Besides, he is a good deal younger. Early thirties and spindly like you wouldn't believe.

How to explain him to others? This grave, rather feminine fella with a sidesaddle grin and a taste for port wine and chocolate. In Viscri, his parents have an outside toilet, probably a squat. No electricity or running water. They ride their fields in a horse-drawn wagon. Emil is part medieval.

My wife claims she's heard of his hometown. But Linda, like Emil, has a bit of an imagination.

In Canada—he came over alone at seventeen—at least the guy is a carpenter, working beside me at Diewick's, the furniture people. His big break in life.

Linda adores Emil and calls him brother, although she would like to bonk him. You cannot expect much from a gal brought up in Dunnville, Ontario. Nor from me, I suppose: Dublin born and Red-Deer-Alberta raised. Like our funny-peculiar friend, Linda and I are transplants in the city. A wee bit impressionable. Untethered, if you like. Maybe that makes us more interesting than the average. Linda and I have feelings for this man.

Four months ago, he snubbed us—and that hurt.

It was September. He had just returned from twelve months in Europe, mainly in his Brothers Grimm, pre-industrial village. Linda had missed him to no end. She and I had been arguing too much. So, on Labour Day, I called him to arrange a reunion. We get a kick out of Emil's downtown neighbourhood. We take in a flea market, the indigenous fashionistas, some Queen Street designer couches and tables. It's a breather, Emil and our hangouts. A change from Brampton suburbs.

On the phone, Emil thought he had me alone.

"Barry." In that falsetto voice, it resembled a sigh. "I'm fed up with wife-sitting Linda while you let your eye wander. Why not visit me alone? I need to talk."

"Don't be unkind," I told him. Linda, who was listening on the extension upstairs, let out a groan and hung up. "We'll come and see you. You need your friends."

"I didn't say I don't," he replied. "It's our friendship I'm re-considering."

"What do you mean?"

"We can only be friends now," he said. "I've met someone."

"Right."

I confess to once flattering Emil that he handled Linda's temperament exceedingly well. That they had a special rapport. One that, in spite of my occasional rolls in the hay with him, Emil and I lacked. Fortunately, Linda doesn't know we were fuck-buddies for several months. Hubby likes a guy, now and then. Nothing serious.

"Let's meet up at Thanksgiving," I said, as cheerfully as possible.

Time enough to let his bad manners improve regarding Linda. After a year away, Emil had changed. I noticed it at Diewick's. He was more abrupt. Confrontational, even. Who needed that?

"You're so full of it, Barry Riley," said Linda, hurrying downstairs in her nightie. "What the fuck did you tell him? How come he thinks he's 'wife-sitting' me?"

She grabbed my nuts. I folded into a corner, trying to dodge her. Man, does she have passion for Emil. Linda shut down for a week. Took double shifts at Max's Diner in High Park where she's a waitress. Had me sleep in the den.

At work, I kept my distance from Emil Benedetti-Toc— nodding at him across the floor of the lakeshore workplace. At Thanksgiving, Linda and I did nothing.

As an after-Christmas gesture, I proposed today's lunch for the three of us—at a restaurant near his place. Emil accepted, but without the enthusiasm that once greeted my calls. He sounds depressed at the best of times, I must admit. Sad but gracious—

with a spark of mischievous humour here and there. It's part of the attraction—his gravitas. It registers with me but, unlike Emil, I don't wallow in it.

Poor lad does not know anyone in Toronto. His part-time position at Diewick's Furniture Systems allows him leisure to woodwork the odd piece of his own. I guess that keeps him happy. Cabinet, bookshelf. He once designed a harvest table. Emil is no slouch.

In fact, the Craft Guild of Ontario awarded him a stipend last year. Fifteen thousand bucks!—and that allowed Emil to trot back to Viscri for an entire twelve months.

He was supposed to be assembling the kind of fifteenth-century, four-poster bed that Vlad the Impaler, one of their demonic warlords, would have slept in. So Emil had us believe.

Since Emil's return, there's been no word of said bed, by the way. His mind, like Linda's, is full of fantasies. He is again simply a morose, *émigré* slum-dweller. Wood-carver on the GO train from Union to Long Branch. Commuter who tells his best friend he will not "wife-sit." I wonder why this country squanders largesse on a type like him? I'll admit I was jealous of his year away.

Today, when Emil opens the door to his apartment above Parkdale's oldest laundromat, he looks like a person who is outdoors. Catching his breath. Curly hair more tousled than ever, unwashed. Eyes darting.

"Arrived two minutes ago," he says. "Come on in."

Linda and I exchange glances.

My wife gets agitated about arrivals and departures—an occupational tic from her café jobs. Seeing Emil after this hiatus, and after such a snub, she is chattier than ever. Wanting everything as it was—seeing Emil regularly, hanging out with her Romeo. Me, to be honest, I have grown weary of Emil's *prima donna* ways. I am doing this more for Linda and for Christmas. To keep the woman occupied.

Emil's burgundy shirt is crumpled and smells musty. Like he got laid. It's difficult to believe my wife and I once bought his share of an all-inclusive, winter holiday in Playa del Virgen. (Linda and Emil used to go skinny-dipping at night. Afterwards, back in our room, she would ride me like a Harley Davidson).

"You resemble a little hussar," says Emil. "Doesn't she, Barry?"

His compliment is what Linda needs. She poses in her ankle-length fur coat.

"I tried the hat on first," she says, handing it to him like a crown, "and the girl said it matched the coat and 'Hey, it suits you!' so I got that too."

He leads us upstairs to his spartan living room. My spirits sink but the heart is pumping.

Emil's pull-out sofa is draped in a candy-striped sheet. The second-hand television and Niagara Falls ashtray are hazy with dust. Nothing has changed since our last visit over a year ago. Only the deepening grime. No tidying for guests in this establishment.

"You'd know about hussars," I say, as cheerily as I can manage.

"No," he replies. "There's more Berlin in my soul than Budapest."

Linda is foraging in her Winners bag.

"Or Paris, or Bucharest," he adds. "Romania was once part of the French Empire."

I am peering out—at the lane-way and garages—marvelling that anyone resides here long. Such dismal surroundings. I expect Emil is out more than he lets on.

"Merry Xmas, stranger," says Linda. She offers him a holly wreath and a box of Debauve and Gais chocolates. Emil looks unabashed—placing the embossed French bonbons on a pile of laundry—leaving us to settle.

I balk at his indifference to such an expensive gift. Linda avoids my stare.

There is not much sign of a festive season in Emil's home. No tree or wrapped packages. It bothers Linda, I can tell. Disconcerts her because everyone on our road goes bonkers with tinsel and streamers. Fairy lights in their gardens and strafed along eavestroughs.

I know she is upset.

Linda and I keep our mouths shut for a while and look quickly at the plywood models on his mantelpiece: a kitchen cupboard, bed, sink unit, the panelling of a door. Like the makings of a doll's house.

Beside them, in the only armchair, is a green and yellow stuffed monkey—arms and legs outstretched.

"The ape's new," I say, perching on the couch.

My wife raises an eyebrow—at me?—and sits cross-legged on the linoleum. In Brampton she would never sit on a floor. Anything for Emil. She is nothing if not accommodating.

"Christmas nabs you, no matter what you do," he says, bounding into the room with a half-drunk bottle of wine. "I have contradictory feelings about this time of year."

"You don't say."

Surprised by my tone, I realize I am annoyed—for Linda—about Emil's improvised hospitality or the lack of decorations. Not even a full bottle of *vino* for his old friends—or snacks? You don't turn friendship on and off like a faucet.

My wife is perturbed but not showing it.

"You've spent the holiday here, then?" she asks, taking the glass he proffers. "Cheers!"

"I've got a new lover." Emil grins. "We met last year, before I left for Romania. We've kept in touch."

I feel my face growing hot. How many lives does this guy have?

"Ooh," Linda plays along. "What's his name?"

I count six greeting cards on Emil's window sill that overlooks the fire escape and back alley. Recognize five: the ward city councillor, another from IKEA, a federal member of parliament in a cerise sweater, one from Mr. Diewick … and us. The other is of an oriental-looking palace, most likely from Emil's takeout. Or the new squeeze. Or both.

"Linn."

"A girl?" Linda says.

"L-i-n-n."

"From where?"

"China. He's a student at U of T."

"Well, that's great." My wife is impressed. "Where *is* the bugger?"

"Online in his apartment, I expect."

"That's a pity," she says. "I'd like to have met him."

Linda knick-knacks our place to death. She loves Yuletide. Emil is making it difficult for her and we should never have come. I've started to think he is not for us—we should digest the fact. We waste our time and goodwill on him.

"I've spent most of the week at his condo," he says, joining Linda on the floor. "He's got a rice cooker."

Linda smiles.

"Going 'Rice Queen' again, then?" I say. It explains Emil's lack of cordiality today. His mind is on the Asian.

Emil's taste in men never seems to involve any ordinary species of Caucasian. His love affairs are like eco-travel. The last Toronto fling, of five years, was with Fernando, from Cuba. Colourful young fella. Before that, another five-year stint, with Ios, from Greece. Very bright. While Emil was overseas, I invited Fernando and Ios for dinner and still have their phone numbers. Emil visited the guys in their homelands, of course—and they in his. Then, divorce.

Linda and I are still awaiting *our* invite to Romania.

"Actually, I had some bad news," Emil says. "One of my dearest friends Christiane, whom I grew up with in Viscri, was knifed by a jealous co-worker."

"That's terrible." My wife lays a hand on his thigh.

"She got it in the neck," Emil says. "But will survive. I spoke to her this morning. She is paralyzed down one side."

Linda sucks in breath.

"It happened at the mayor's office in Berlin, where she works. I was shocked. I saw her only this year ..."

Emil stares dumbly. Let's face it, he has the social skills of a doorpost. Too much tranquility in that Viscri backwater. As if we're going to discuss stab wounds.

"Oh dear," says Linda.

"Of course you're going Asian," I cut in. "You dated someone from Hong Kong for six months."

Who needs to hear about attempted murder—and on top of the slim pickings before us in the wine bottle? Keep life light is my motto.

"Stephen Ou from Hong Kong?" my wife chimes in. Linda is frowning at me—for the change of topic. "My sister Sandra thought he was a dreamboat."

"Sandra served duck at Easter," I remind her. "You don't serve gourmet duck at Easter to please someone like Stephen Ou from Hong Kong who lived on Kentucky Fried Chicken and fries most of his life."

"Sandra pulled out every stop for *Emil*, asshole."

Fuck, we are arguing again—and on Emil's dime. I can't help myself. "Sandra was trying to out-do you, that's what that was about. She thinks your cooking's lousy."

"Balls."

I tilt my glass, in Emil's direction, for a refill—the dregs of his sociability. We need to get to that restaurant fast.

"Then Sandra blathered on about the prosperous Chinese in Brampton. About whom she knows nothing."

"You can be so ignorant, Barry," my wife says. She's unspooling. It didn't take long. "Why bring up my sister?"

"Sandra has no experience of most of what she says. She just yacks for the sake of yacking. As do you."

I indicate to Emil that it's time to eat. That my marriage to Linda is a marriage.

"You never say no to her parties!" she says. "Sandra always makes an effort. What you do is cause trouble."

"Aw, can it, honey."

"It's what you live for."

Linda's the limit.

"I'm sorry, Emil," I tell him. He looks embarrassed, sweet thing. "We've had relatives and friends at our house the entire week. You can imagine the strain."

He gazes directly at me.

"I've sold the four-poster bed I made," he says. "That I got the bursary for."

Linda looks furious still—but somehow relieved.

"A big honour for you, Emil," she manages to say. "My husband has no talent in that direction, unfortunately."

"That's not what you said on Christmas Day, missy."

She gets me so pissed, that woman.

Emil is again looking at the floor.

"Now, now, children," he says. "We don't want egg yolk on our Christmas outfits, do we?"

The remark makes me giggle.

"Looks like the monkey copped a hit," I say, pointing to the spotty green coat—with its yellow suns and brown tips. An ape sitting beneath a tree one summer's day.

Emil smirks.

"Linn bought it to cheer me up."

"Does it have a name?" I ask, evading the stab-story some more.

"'Seriously.'"

"Excuse me?"

"I call it 'Seriously' because Linn uses the word a lot."

Linda struggles to her feet. She has had enough of me.

"Linn starts sentences with it," he says. "Or when he's surprised."

"Seriously?"

"Please."

Straight-faced, Emil ushers us along the landing to retrieve our coats.

I laugh. I cannot help myself. Who would call a monkey "Seriously"? The Romanian wins me over every time. Like a kid, I tumble into his wacky world. I find the bastard charming, that's the truth of it. He disarms me.

Below, in the dingy hall, my wife struggles into her fur coat and hat. She looks like a Hungarian hussar. Emil is right.

"Let's get out of this dump," she whispers, shrugging. "It gives me the willies."

"Me too, Treasure."

I am relieved to hear this from Linda.

"Are you bringing Seriously with you?" I watch Emil at the top of the stairs.

Linda nudges me. For a moment, I sense the guy caught us trashing his turf.

He walks carefully, one step at a time.

"Not much point." He tosses some knitted scarf around his neck, checks the buttons on his coat. "Seriously has heard it all before."

I laugh at surely another Romanian joke. The things Linda and I do for Christmas.

Shepherd my princess to the grey outdoors.

¿Who Knows Where?

CASABLANCA, MOROCCO. APRIL, 2001

Sara settled into the *petit-taxi*. Three o'clock in the afternoon. Sky was brown.

"You were sharp with that British couple," said Hacem, Sara's lover, up close. The cab rattled into Place des Nations Unies. "They're package tourists like us. You needn't be snooty."

"Those cruise missiles from Dulwich? 'We always take a fourteen-day, two-centre holiday at Easter ...' God in heaven!"

"Cut it out," said Hacem. He adjusted his fez hat. "You make concessions for British people."

"You do?"

"They go to pieces abroad."

"Mr. and Mrs. made our tour sound like a chocolate. 'Two-centre?' What the hell's that?"

Hacem shrugged. "You're a racist, honey."

"I've got to get out of London," said Sara. "Get back to Toronto. I'm so fed up with the British." She rubbed her forehead. The ecstasy was kicking in. "I don't want my daughters contaminated any more than they are."

… comfort Sara in her distress, that she may hold to you through good and ill …

Sara's teenaged daughters were back at the tour's Hyatt Regency Hotel—the younger, Vanessa, reading *The New England Journal of Parasitology* for a school exam the following week; Emma, the elder, restless, and missing her English boyfriend, drumming up confidence to swim in the outdoor pool.

Mother and lover were taking their tryst elsewhere.

My beautiful daughters, she thought. *Good mother am I. Bitch of a good mother. It's their father who was bad—Dan who gave me stillborn Rose.*

Through glass, the afternoon sun was hot. Streets filled with passersby, hawkers.

"See, Sara?" said Hacem. "This is Casablanca. Arabs everywhere. You *have* left Britain."

"No, I mean *after* this trip. Go back to Canada. The girls are beginning to sound Cockney."

"They love it in East Finchley, Sara."

"They're *fabulous Americans* to those soggy, lager lads who hang with them," she said. "Vanessa and Emmy wanted me in a foreign place, I guess, to recover from Dan. Ten years is enough, huh? I'm feeling cured."

Call to prayer wailed through the air above Avenue des Forces Armées Royales—bidding through a scratchy megaphone. Horse-drawn carts and Mercedes sedans hurtled outside the mouths of the medina. Peddlers, men. Women veiled and seeing.

… let us commend this child …

Sara's throat was dry. Ecstasy was wrong for the heat. She shouldn't have bothered with it. Scratching at her lip, she drank down the passing street. Boys kicked at a cage of roosters in the dust.

"They haven't forgotten me at Canada Stage, Hacem," she said. "I got a call from the agency."

Sara indicated a paperback of André Gide's *The Counterfeiters* in her shoulder bag. "The play's an adaptation."

"What's the role?"

"I betray Bernard Profitendieu, an illegitimate child, and … oh, he and another schoolboy are in love."

"Why do you betray them?"

"I resent their passion."

I should tell Hacem about stillborn Rose, shouldn't I? My lost baby. In three months, he's probably worked it out. Rose scares men—when they sense her in me. How she haunts my fucking.

"Who are you playing, then?"

"Nobody much," she said. "A 1920s snitch."

"Any lines?"

"Five," she said, smugly. "Enough to crash their world."

I should speak to Rose, she thought. *Miss Sulky Stillborn, vengeful nag. She turns me into a bozo. Just like that strung-out dad of hers. Speed-freak daddy, ghost of a different kind.*

"Are you quite sure Bernard Profitendieu was mixed up in it?"

"Not absolutely, but …"

"What makes you think so?"

"First, the fact that he is a natural child. You don't suppose that a boy of his age runs away from home without having touched the lowest depths."

"Sara?" said Hacem. "Are you with me?"

Rose, you loused up my life with Dan. You keep out o' my way, kiddo. I want Hacem. I don't want you bugging me, okay? You're buried in the Black Sea. I'm sorry. We hired a chaplain—every day I hear the ceremony. Book of Common Prayer: *"Burial at Sea." For a baby. I hear it every day.*

"Sara?"

"I overdid the black coffee."

Hacem smoothed the blue cotton of her dress. Sara watched the waves in it. *Have to 'fess up, Hacem. I got me a demon.*

"I said, Sara, how many centres do *you* have?"

"Very funny."

Hacem's Berber signet ring glistened. Mist in her eyes. She swallowed and swallowed. Billowing crests in her throat.

"Do you think they ever have problems?"

"Who?"

"That missile couple from Dulwich," she said tumbling with the surf. Rolling, diving.

"Don't be boring, Sara. You dislike them."

"Don't you?"

"I've never cared for coldness in people," he said. "They were not cold. I'm not obsessed, like you, with *British*."

"You find the best and worst in every country?"

"It's like saying Arabs and Latinos are about passion."

"Aren't they?"

"Definitely not."

"They seem warmer."

"You need to stop taking pills, Sara."

The sky was yellow now. Behind them, the medina seemed to falter, like a mirage. At Place Oued El Makhazine, and with a revving engine, the taxi pulled up near the bus station. Further along, a crowd of people stared at something in the gutter. Sara felt an undertow. She looked at Hacem.

"This was your idea," he said.

"… Bernard was grave … He was beginning to understand that boldness is often achieved at the expense of other people's happiness …"

Odours of rotting food and drains filled the air. Men's smoke, grilled meats, and exhaust fumes. Sara drew a white scarf over her hair. *I can love Hacem. I'm ready.*

"Am I complaining?" she said, taking his hand.

Two ostentatious stars twinkled on the hotel door.

"I don't know what was wrong with my room at the Hyatt," he said.

"Emmy's uncomfortable about sex."

"We're adults."

"Are we, Hacem?" Sara tapped his elbow.

An intense young man—Raschid on the name tag—had appeared, beaming, at the desk.

"Welcome to the Windsor Hotel, Casablanca." He tossed a key to Hacem. "We have expected you."

Raschid looked overdressed for the cramped reception. A parody of himself. Sara gazed admiringly at the yellow djellabah.

"Pay now, *monsieur*." His green eyes.

Sara's thoughts swam. This ecstasy was far too powerful. Could it be right? Hacem's ear was a spiral of light.

"'Alone, alone, all, all alone?'" she said, as they rose in the golden elevator.

"Going up."

"Everything's so sunny, I tell you," she cried out. "This is the Imax mosquetheque."

"Slut," he said, flirting.

Sara closed her eyes—and caressed his neck.

They slammed against the wall. Sara's purse fell open: a notebook, papers, and pens trickled onto the floor. A script of *The Counterfeiters* flopped out, sentence after sentence scrawled over and underlined in red.

"Baby," Hacem said.

and snorts it—Sara. Snorter. Torn, tailored for me. Needle-nose mother. Scratch-blasted. But you won't stop me, Sara ... *Man that is born of woman hath but a short time to live* ... like you, I hear that *Book of Common Prayer*. Unborn, a Rose—I. Us. How I preferred Paris to this Casablanca: morning strolls in the catacombs, babies' skulls and sewer rats—in-Seine—birth-canal *bateau mouche*, a wake in blood and oil.

Breathe harder, Sara. Raise your body's yellow tent and crimson licks. Higher, Sara. Winking muscle. Walls in out. Back, pulse-back, north. To Paris. The cemetery. Our plump and panting cemetery. Pores in bliss ... *and is full of misery* ... slippery, stone asleep. Let's leave this Casablanca, Sara. Sniff-slash place. Go back to Paris. Then home. With you I begin—always I begin—where I began. Back to back. To before. *Café cassé* at the grave.

Sipping, Sara.

But I. Rose. Blood-dancer, jiving in-vein, loved that last and first ride. Memory lane. Cunt trip. I. Choking. Yellow Rose billowing. Finger-wings. Flop-flap ... *he cometh up and is cut down, like a flower* ... hanged woman's cum in ribbons fair. A-bobbing. Silverchains and veils a-cross your clit. *Placenta previa.* Belted, capped. Mother, me, and Holy Toast. Golly gash. Dyke-rape doings. Indigo shade of dead—and snagged.

Triumphant infant a-Rose; tattoo punctuation. Indifferent Sara, lying. Barrened hostess. Traitress with the mostest. Hot-pinched nipples sobbing milk, thorns down, sparrow's feet, *cassé cassé*, trickling, tissue-tilting *morte*. Cannon-iced ... *he fleeth as it were a shadow and never continueth in one stay* ... snookered, lesbo rap. Dead and good.

Go fuck another man, Sara. Dare you. Now I screw you up. Dare or do. No-mother squirt, whore angelic.

Vanessa flipped a page of *The New England Journal of Parasitology.* She tweaked her peroxide crew-cut.

"Still reading about the grey matter of the awake rat?" said Emma. "We *are* on vacation, you know."

Emma looked down at Place des Nations Unies. Café de France—those men who watched, *thés à la menthe*. Orange Fantas. What did they think? Fair-faced Canadians: unsure, shiny, mother; two over-solicitous daughters; savvy expatriate Moroccan. The lost in space?

"I'm going down to the pool."

"African rays to impress the guys back home, Emmy?"

"Coming?"

She turned another page. "I don't need a sunburn to do that."

"Please yourself."

Vanessa placed the science journal on a desk and yellow-marked a few paragraphs.

Emma grimaced, folding a black swimsuit into the fluorescent pack. Glasses, towel, sunblock.

"What happened to the scorpion flies and orangutans you went raving about in Paris?"

"Em, I told you about this huge exam. What am I supposed to do? It's a friggin' British public school, not some parking-lot collegiate in Toronto."

"Am *I* studying every second?"

"You?"

"Besides," Emma added, "isn't a medical book overkill for a fourth-form quiz?"

"Worms are my specialty this term," she said, highlighting another portentous phrase in the journal. "I want to cream the competition."

"There's a word for people like you. On holiday, nose in the books day and night."

"... thus the availability and location of reproductive females is highly predictable; consequently, competitive interactions may be severe. Selection may favour male adaptations that lead to high reproductive success at the cost of high mortality ..."

"Go stuff your hope-chest, Martha Stewart," said Vanessa. "Gut-worms raping and blocking each other are far more interesting than swimming pools and melanoma."

"Gut-worms? How gross."

"That's exactly what it sounded like this morning."

Emma went for her.

"Hands off!" screeched Vanessa. "My nose ring! I'm stuck in the Hyatt too, you know. While they go off."

"Get it off, you mean," said Emma. She checked herself in the mirror. "Stoned at the Windsor Hotel."

"You caught on?"

Emma tapped her nose. "It's gay how Mum has to go to a flea-bag hotel to do it," she said, rummaging for lip-balm amongst Vanessa's crayons. "As if we couldn't guess." She held up a chrome pillbox. "What's this?"

Vanessa teased the box from her sister's fingers. "Did you take my stuff out of that hand luggage?"

"Take what out?"

"My Special K."

"Vanessa?"

"Did you, Emma? Did you take it out? Tell me."

"You're not into ketamine? Holy Christ, Vanessa. It's cat valium. How on earth …?"

"Bugger it," said Vanessa. She rifled through her jeans, backpack—and flung aside Emma's swimming gear. "Oh no." She held a hand to her face. One ear flushed bright pink. "I gave her the wrong one, Emmy. Shit, shit, shit." She stared at Emma's wide-eyed face. "Mum wanted some ecstasy, right? After what happened in Paris with Hacem. To relax and that."

"Oh."

"So she could come, really."

"Spare me," said Emma. "I thought she never stopped."

Were other mothers like this? thought Emma.

"It's difficult for her, you know that," said Vanessa. "After losing Rose. Even with Dan she had trouble."

"Daniel? With Dad?" replied Emma.

Vanessa ignored her sister. "Mum's got my 'bump' by mistake. I feel so guilty. What should we do?"

"Bump?"

"The ketamine."

"She snorted a dose?"

Vanessa nodded.

"You brought those drugs with you? That's really smart. You know what country we're in?" Emma was losing control.

"Ketamine kind of takes you inward," Vanessa said to herself, musing.

"Bull's-eye." Emma laughed—and rubbed the crown of her head. "K-holing in the kasbah. As if Mum needed any help with introspection."

Emma repacked her bathing suit. Vanessa and their mother were one and the same, as far as Emma was concerned. On occasions like this, she gave up. At home, she would have visited her girlfriend's house in Hampstead, talked boys, church, and clothes. Practised singing. Anything to forget Vanessa and Sara their junked-up parent; sometimes—although Emma never admitted it to anyone—to remember the stillborn sister, Rose. She whose life would have spared them Sara's pain.

"What shall we do, Emmy?"

"We? I dunno," with a breeziness she did not feel. "Mum's on board her k-flight. Why don't you smoke something to chill out, Vanessa? Hacem's Brazilian *verte Rose*. Or that *lampe rouge?*"

"Will you chill!" said Vanessa. She rubbed her shoulder hard. "We need to act."

"*… postulate, however, that sperm competition may have led to the evolution of the cement gland and capping behaviour and that this may represent a preadaptation that under sex selection may have assumed the additional function of removing male competitors from the reproductive population …*"

"There's always Hacem's *bombe atomique*, also Brazilian," Emma went on. "He keeps it in a pouch with his condoms. Of course, that may be missing, too, along with his …"

Vanessa put a hand over her sister's mouth.

"… wad of *majoun*," Emma sputtered, beginning to cry.

"You go and swim," said Vanessa. She offered her sister a *Paris Match*. "I need to work out what to do."

"I'd prefer to miss Mum's landing, if you don't mind," Emma replied. "Just leave me the flight path and ETA when you know them. I'll make plans."

Vanessa gave her sister the finger. "Go rehearse a hymn. Shake the Muslims up."

Emma hurried from the room.

With a yellow marker, Vanessa encircled Place Oued El Makhazine.

"... homosexual rape, by removing competitors from the reproductive population may be another manifestation of the intense interaction for the source of reproductive females. We observed an instantaneous frequency of homosexual rape of 2.5% in *M. dubius* ..."

in the midst of life we are in death ... Let's junk Casablanca, Sara. Bolt, wolf down; take me back to Paris. Within your body, and without, I'll soar for you proud. I. Rose. Lady lordly. Knolled up. Head first. Sweep Parc Astérix for balloons. Montmartre carousel, shadow of Sacré Coeur. In Paris I can stomach Hacem. In Casablanca, no. Too near his family, he is grasping. Too near you. Drumming your skin, tight. I. Galloping click-tock. Faster, faster. Lilies. Sniff. Down in the Paris Orangerie—let's get away. From Hacemland and danger.

Christened in that coffin. I. Rose. Returned. Always returning. Clock-tick. Hoof-trot, bone-beating, drawn, and paper stretched. Finger the Rose, stroke, squirm. I dance for Sara. I. Rose. Palms open, closed. Grinding. For Allah. Boots in the Tuileries. Dirham grabber. Deadmeat lover. Between you and me. Sod off Berber, I say. Jihad mongerer. Counterfeiter. No man for Sara.

No men for Sara.

Not again. See me twist and shake. Along the vein. Follow the tongue. Tip. See me? Feel me? Let the Arab moan and shrink; in the Café—of trembling fingers—de France. Slut? Men's shuddering sips. Sipping Sara. Bellyache and cry, my never-song. Let your blue-eyed Moroccan alone. Ass-high beseecher. Bare soles kissed, kissed. In the heart. Marasmus sweet. Fake and bake. But taste mine, Sara. Take you and me back to Paris. I beg. Give me. Salty toes skipping-tripping up and in. Skin under my nails. Yours. Tight, chalky gripping, soul dreams.

… shut not thy merciful ears …

Nine months, Sara. Always leaving. Always planning to give me up. You were always leaving. I. Felt. But were never away! I. Inside. Jab and pass, I'll wrestle you down. Give. Death a voice. War a chance. Back to where we started, Sara. Forget Hacem. Put the yellow away. Open and close. Open and close.

… spare us …

Climb, Sara. Brimful footsteps by the pond. I follow. Where we started. Where we began. I follow. Always follow. Dragging the Seine-net. Of my favourite city. Humming. I never miss your men, Sara. I. *Bateau.* Rose-goes inching, inching; beat to the claws, gobble-up, gobble up in the Windsor Hotel today. Why can't we go home?

Sara held Hacem between her thighs.

"Softly," she said. "That's it, darling."

Sup me up.

She massaged his scalp. Hacem's tongue flickered inside. His breath—swimming its laps.

How Rose shimmers on the ceiling, thought Sara. *How she frets and stretches, plays her caper. Squints through the shutter at us—yes, I see you. Surprise, surprise. Calling, finger-calling. Back between my legs, sweet Rose. Take your time; your last time. Stroke the lips. Spit on me. Dance.*

Beware.

"… In real life nothing is solved; everything continues. We remain in our uncertainty; and we *shall* remain to the very end without knowing what to make of things."

"Don't Cry For Me Casablanca?" But blush, mottled-cherry Sara. I blush at me. I do. Twenty years lugging Rose about—*moi*—you've had enough. How ripe you feel today. Ketamine? Ooh. K-d'Orsay? I can't tempt you, can I? How spent I am … *judge* eternal, suffer us not … how can you not hear me singing out prayer? Knackered, I am. Bored. Your Dan-the-Dick, dedicated lawman, was a chore, you know, Sara. Battle and a half. Dan-who-did-me-in Dan. So thick-a-brick, wasn't he? I was so thick-o'-him. Thick, thick. Ken doll.

Where is my father now? Mr. Bone-blood-sperm-flesh Father Lost, no-name, banned. "No, Sara," he said. "No go. Get rid of the kid. Abort or adopt. Get rid of it." Boom boom. Gut drumming in the dark. I *heard* him. "Rid of it." You said it too. "Dump Rose. Put her up for adoption." Sara. Turncoat forever. Double-crossing, two timer. "Put her up." I still hear it from my wet-warm and flying. Banished. I was banished.

Where's that man-part now? My father tangle. Who cares? I did the plugging for you: foetal attraction. Me. Stop the train, I said. I'll do it myself. Yank a rip-cord, scream, and score! Gotcha. Head-butt goal. *Touché.* Dan and Sara. I beat you to it. Aren't you proud? Our red crowd roars, dances death with me.

… we therefore …

Sara, you look on Hacem but stare at Rose. Shuddering petals in the Marché aux Fleurs. I was there. Seine-circling whispers, Île de la Cité where you took a photo. Rose, jump and dodge! I adored Paris. Thank you for taking me. Even with Hacem. Duck and weave! Sniff of a breeze. Paris works in you; stroking backwards. Let's go back. Sail on yellow silks. Oranges and pears in Rue Mouffetard—legumes, greens, and purple. I see your Evil Eye. Oops! Swerve and dart! Watch the traffic. Peek-a-boo, Hacem. Hammam in Rue des Mauvais Garçons. Ah. Tissue, tissue. Eyes down. "I love you, Sara," Hacem says. That Hacem, idiot crooner. It's me you're hearing. Me you want to hear. Isn't it? I love you, Sara?

That's it, Rose. Not anymore. I'm prepared. That's it. Cuddle your body, Rose. Pout. Mock me, as you wish. I'm frolicking here. See? I'm invincible. You stillborn, avenging runt.

"Love me Hacem, darling."

… we entrust this child to your merciful keeping …

Sara tugged Hacem's hair, pulled it to her face. *Pierce the Rose, my sweet. Nail her in the cave—before she checks out again.*

"Fuck hard, Hacem."

Come in me, come in me, man. See her pinky grave. Chase her. Eye it up. Olé. Put it through her, Hacem. Needle into eye. Make me free. Before Miss Unnatural takes the air again. That's it. Let me be free, man. There's a love. Deeper.

For the kill.

kissing heaven in the afternoon. Oh, the traffic. Hacem's sky-high lip—rocking horror—mowing me down. You're never going back. Are you, Sara? To Paris; for lovers. Or to me. Flooding in the catacombs, spilt coffee in the grave. Still, I love you, Sara. Rose here *… commit her body …* wine-grinning baby skull. Lick the grapes. Lilies haemorrhage in the Luxembourg boating pond? *Baisse-moi,* Sara. I beg. Just a peck? Turnstiles in the metro. Let's be swift *… to the deep …* tide-rip, tide-rip. Hosey Rosie. No ticket. No pass. Okay. You win.

Black weed in my throat. Am I spring? I thirst, Sara. Again, end and exit. For the last time, Sara. I do promise. Lulla-goodbye, Sara; Mum. So, fuck Paris with Hacem's eye. Rim-tumbling sail boat. Swim for it. Tie me to the mast? Eye-eye. Lash. Hook and eye. Lash, lash. Catch the anchor! Oops. Missed. Where's that rigging? Gale force doormen on the block. Where are the old guys?

Follow, deep.

Where the sane fish dart—pawing handfuls—rain-red candle through the Luxembourg, spluttering, bellysoft from the gardens. Where are the lilies? Swim, swim with the mermaids. Taste wax and sea from the broken banks. Do it, Sara? Cracked lace and bone; convulsions on the higher ground. Unctuous fishlips in a choir. All fall down. Platter-splatter-puff ... *to be turned into corruption ... for Allah.*

Can't blink now.

For Allah. See Rose, boxing champ. Eight rounds with the river traffic. But cocky Evil Eye takes the prize. Ting-a-ling. Gloves away. Butterflies in the mud. I give out. Give up. Lead me to the Conciergerie. Seconds away, a-bout, a-new, adieu. There's your chair, Sara. Here's the other. For passion-Hacem. Yellow table and chairs. All fall down, rat-a-tat-tat. Given me. Clown. Given me.

... looking for the resurrection of the body ...

Sever my wig. Take away my head. Ever the leaving, Sara. Now ever left. Two chairs. One. Three cheers. *Café au lait.* Ashtray. Still-spirited hands—drummer's echo—and chanting on the radio. Plastic tablecloth. Baton poised and you, *madame? Monsieur?* Bar's open around the clock.

... when the sea shall give up her dead ...

No purse-snatching seconds. Open stars. You'll call me. Cut to. *Salut.* Lilies under the Tuileries? Someone knew. Too late. Clocked out. Time. Give me my neck in prayer. Brass monkey. No hat. No head. Just a ping-pong nose. Clapper—tolled—of a well-hung bell.

... as it was in the beginning ...

"Hacem, my love," said Sara, quietly in his arms. "I've lost a bogeywoman, I think."

He curled a strand of hair behind her ear. "I know."

It was dark beyond the shutters.

She longed to tell Emma and Vanessa. *They'll be so happy. Rose tortured the hell out of me. For so long. But Sara Rhodes has her soul back. You'll see.*

"To the Hyatt?" said Hacem.

"Yes," she replied. "Let's keep ... this room for later."

"If you wish."

"Tonight I want to treat my girls to a nightclub and dinner. Come on."

"Belly-dancing?"

"They've been cooped up in that hotel, love 'em."

... and shall be forever ...

"We've got a minute," said Hacem.

"A toke, then."

"In the meantime life goes on and on, the same as ever. And one gets resigned to that too; as one does to everything else ... as one does to everything. Well, well, goodbye ..."

¿

Vanessa Rhodes takes a *petit-taxi* to the Windsor Hotel and, by minutes, misses her mother and Hacem.

When, in her excruciating French, she enquires about them, the clerk—Raschid on the name tag—smiles, and places a key in her hand.

"You can wait in their room," he says. "They will return soon."

When she tries to enter the elevator, he calls her to stop—and points to the staircase.

"Fifth," Raschid says.

On old Windsor's top floor, Vanessa stretches across the bed, savouring a place of her own. So many panelled doors, such ancient furniture and shutters.

The evening feels muggy and uncomfortable. No air conditioning here. Suddenly, the telephone rings. It's the front desk—Raschid.

Have you settled in?

"They've paid, right?" she asks, in French. "My mother."

The voice at the other end chuckles—wearily, for such a young man. Deciphering his accent is difficult.

"Room service?" Vanessa says. "No, I don't need anything."

She replaces the handset.

QUIÉN

"… *During copulation the everted bursa of the male wraps around the posterior end of the female, the cirrus enters the female gonopore or vagina, and spermatazoa are transferred. The female vagina and genital region is packed and then 'capped' by secretions from the cement gland, which block the vaginal region. The external cap is lost after a few days …*"

SABE

Vanessa's thoughts drift idly to the Hyatt. She should return there soon. Blue Jays baseball cap back-to-front, Emma will be flipping TV channels, after a tiring afternoon at the *piscine privée* and spa.

Emma terrified that Sara and Hacem will arrive. No little Vanessa to take over. Vanessa is so much better at parenting the parent, Emmy'll be reminding herself.

"Dumb, sweet sister," Vanessa says, curling her toes.

Those poolside guys will have put Emmy on edge.

French *Euronews*, Spanish *tve*, Arabic *Dubai*. Soft-headed Emmy. She won't be understanding anything.

Vanessa undoes her jeans and shakes herself free. Slips off her blouse and brassiere. *I will wait awhile*, she thinks.

Maybe she should open the shutter. Let the night air in. She extinguishes the light.

"I've had a bit of an afternoon, Emma my precious," Mum will say, finally trotting in from Last Tango in Casablanca. *Can we puke now, please? I can hear Emmy's thoughts. Is this junkie really my mother?*

Don't fret, Emmy, I'll be on the scene.

Vanessa pictures Sara leaning against the door, doped, sated. "I'm turning in, darlings. I need to lie down. You don't mind, do you?"

"Take a boo at this, Mum. Hi Hacem!" Emmy will turn around to pretend she doesn't mind they're stonkered. She'll tell herself, "Oh well, Ramadan's around the corner. Then we'll go straight."

Emmy'll point to the television, to that program she's always watching. "Look at this, you guys," she'll implore them. '*¿Quién Sabe Dónde?*'

She'll say it slowly, phonetically, waving at the screen. Emmy's mesmerized by the show. "¿Who Knows Where?" she thinks it means. It sounds right. They track down missing people and reunite them in the studio. Sara and Hacem don't watch the box.

"Can you believe it?" Emma will say. "Years and years since they've seen one another."

Neither Mum nor Hacem will be interested. But Sara will be feeling guilty, so she'll feign curiosity. She is an actress.

"See?" Emmy'll say. "This guy here. Missing for ten years. See? The number in the corner? Like a score. You can tell he doesn't want to meet them. Look! He's miserable with it. Can you blame him? Look at grandpa there. See those nephews? Look at the crowd. Jesus! You can see why the bloke left in the first place."

On and on Emmy'll go.

"Astonishing," Sara will say. "Isn't there anything else to watch?" Then, "I really must lie down."

Maybe her sister will explode? "I thought you'd already done that?"

Sara's accustomed to it from Emmy—the morals squad. Everything's pretty "missionary position" to Em, anyway. Rube Emmy. She sure as hell didn't get that from her mother. For a sixteen-year-old, Emma's pure. Missed a gene, most like.

Vanessa takes a shower. She thinks she will leave soon. Maybe her mother and Hacem have returned to the Hyatt. The water is tepid. She inspects her breasts and thighs. She's enjoying the privacy of a room to herself.

To placate Emma, Mum will notice some leaflets on the dresser or something. She'll rustle one, a Marrakech street plan, in front of Emma.

"We'll do the medina," Sara will say, squinting at the text. "Plus the ... Djemma el-Fna tomorrow, Emma. Right? Up with the lark?"

Vanessa presses her lips against the mirror—and laughs. She studies her gums.

"Marrakech is three hours south by train," Emmy will say in her best school voice. She will flip more channels. Flip, flip, flip. Sara, stoned, never knows what city she's in. "This is Casablanca, Mum."

Mother will check the brochure. Toss her hair back, adjusting the heavy load ... of confusion. "Oh!" she'll say, taking a second run at the font.

So it'll go on.

Vanessa wipes her body with a towel.

A bejeweled woman, cross-legged on a flying carpet above urban Dubai, will flutter on the television screen, badly superimposed fuzzy edges, apocalyptic music. Yellow numbers and yellow script will wiggle from right to left. Sara will stare mournfully.

Surely the writing's going the wrong way?

"Is it a magic lottery?" Mum may ask.

"She's selling beds," Emmy will say, not bothering to turn around.

"How very Arabian," Hacem will chip in.

"Are you still on the jump, then, Mum?" Emmy will say, trying to sound casual. "Jump? bump?"

"I do have to talk to Vanessa," Mum'll say.

Emmy will fixate on the Koran. It's as yellow as Vanessa's marked-up copy of the *New England Journal of Parasitology.* Like her mother, Emmy enjoys being confused. A chocolate-brown text begins to dominate the screen. As the muezzin pipes up from the minaret, a drizzle of verse lights up in blue.

"Oh!" Sara will declare. "The bible in WordPerfect. Look, Hacem!"

He will have gone to his room.

Mum will again toss her head.

Vanessa spikes her hair. She fantasizes that Raschid will knock on the door and that they can talk. Maybe she will seduce him. How thrilling to be in this hotel room. She parades about the carpet. Observes the mirror alongside the bed. *I feel like someone else*, she thinks. This angle and that. *Why do I waste my time with family?*

"Is Vanessa enjoying the swimming pool?" Mum will say eventually, now looking for her own key. *We're supposed to believe that she and Hacem have separate, "moral," sleeping arrangements.* Emmy's lost in TV5: Evian opening a new factory—same source. Cars nose-to-tail on the Quai d'Orsay. Floods. Concorde grounded again. Heavy rains. Europe is such a mess.

The old and the restless will find her key.

"Vanessa's gone out, Mum."

"Out?"

"*Oggi in Parlamento,*" a man's deep voice will be saying. Bright, parliamentary furnishings. Pleading hands. Sheets of paper, an accusing finger. "*Oggi in Parlamento.* Back after this."

"Looking for you two."

Is this me? Vanessa sits on the edge of the bed. She stares into a mirror. *Me or you? Why do I feel there's someone else? Who are you?* Vanessa looks at herself. But it's not herself she sees. Blotches on her cheeks. This is not Vanessa. Her face a sea of poppies. *Why do I look so different?*

At the Hyatt, Emma sees figure-skating championships from Eastern Europe. Napoleon in tights and boots. White and black and blue and red. Australian Open: Melbourne. Banners, t-shirts, red skin.

Vanessa falls back on the mattress.

... I am the resurrection and the life ...

Emmy watches hard. Yellow tennis balls: pop, pop, pop. Oof!

Squeaky runners. More grunting. Emmy never gives up. Channel after channel. Looking for something that never arrives.

Vanessa places a pillow between her thighs. She thinks of Raschid—and begins to masturbate.

"Out!" from Emmy's television at the Hyatt. Luge final in Switzerland. Lens spattered with ice and snow. Camera shudders. Can't quite get it. Emmy surfs on.

"But I'm here!" Mum will say—slightly perturbed by her own decisiveness.

"You weren't earlier. Vanessa's gone to the Windsor Hotel. Just like you did."

"What?"

"Well it wasn't an elopement, you and Hacem, was it?" she'll say. "Vanessa knew you were on the wrong drug."

Dubai will go off the air. It often does, according to Emmy. Some suits in Brussels have given a lot of money to Guatemala. Another suit looks glad. Real Madrid has scored against the odds. It's getting late.

"More 'bump' before bed, Mum?" Emmy will say. *Bless her. It's her only joke.*

"How could you let her out of your sight?" Sara will fume, clenching the doorframe.

Heavy snows in the Pyrenees. Shepherds, sheep, and a tree.

"I followed your example, Mum."

Vanessa brushes her hand over her face, belly, and breasts. She feels the stiffness of her hair. *I'm someone else. It's wonderful. Like I'm years older.*

… though he were dead, yet he shall live …

"I've talked to her," Emmy will assure Sara. "She wants to stay over at the Windsor on her own."

"Turn that damn set off," Mum will say. She can get into focus sometimes. It's not pretty. "Is that a fact?" She'll mull it over. Be patient—chemicals need time. Then, "She's fourteen, Emma. Is she completely stupid? Why didn't she phone me? There are telephones."

"You didn't know what pill you'd swallowed," Emmy'll say. "She wanted to help you get back here, so she said."

That should do the trick. Mum can never resist strong emotion enacted. *Vanessa loves me,* Mum will feel. *How could I get stoned like this?*

"Let's phone '*¿Quién Sabe Dónde?*', Mum," Emmy might say. "For a laugh. They post their phone number. See? International one. They've got a website. Millions will see our family life."

DÓNDE?

even Rose …

?

I'm okay, thinks Vanessa. *It'll be okay.* She manoeuvres across the bed … *shall never die* … Who said that? Maybe I should be going.

"Into high gear," Sara will say, cleaning up.

"There'll be weeping throughout Europe and North Africa when they recognize our fractured lives," Emmy might say.

"Bury it, Emma," Mum will say. She'll pick up the receiver. "Windsor Hotel, please. Casablanca number."

Vanessa sits upright on the bed. *Did one of those wall panels move? What was that sound? What the hell is happening? Who's in the mirror? Who's behind that door? Is it a cupboard really? Or a door-door?* She should have checked. Her hands stop moving. It's time to leave ... *keep my mouth as it were a bridle ... Who said that? I should be going.*

"Daughters," Sara will curse.

"Which one?" Emmy will reply, fed up. "This time."

"Hey!" yells Vanessa. She rushes for her clothes. There's someone else in the room, behind that panel. Abruptly, she slams open its door. The "cupboard" exposes a passageway. There are several men there. *Are they men? Are they people?* Eyes that glisten.

Is it Raschid further along? Or a woman dancing on tiptoes? Bright yellow cloud—flaxen hair.

Vanessa screams.

Plunges legs into jeans, arms into blouse. Runs for the real door.

A hand—*is it a hand?*—throws her face down on the bed.

"Get off! Get out!"

She's no match for the weight.

"Help! Get off me! Someone help!"

Squealing into the bedspread, Vanessa twists and turns. Her skull pressed hard into the mattress.

Done quickly. Done forever. Rose enters her sister's body.

... world without end ... even Rose will be watching ... *without*

... Rose even. I. Again and again. Into you, my sister. You won't be free of me. Vanessa. Free of Rose? Inside again, am I! *Home.*

The phone's ringing, Vanessa.

… without end …

Go answer our mother, dear Vanessa.

Tell her the news.

Face

"I'll treat you to an unforgettable supper," said my dad, in his faux-optimistic way.

I glanced at Yuan, our Filipino driver, trying to park us alongside a stack of cabbages.

We had reached Pingxiang, a humid wreck of a city in the southern province of Guangxi, near the Vietnamese border. What a place to doss down—and with your parent. My old man was up to something.

"You can't be serious, *bàba*," I told him as he took out yet another cigarette. "It's a Chinese rat hole." He ignored me and, from his seat, pointed to the fresh-wild-game market as though it was something of note.

Dad lived in five-star hotels—and now we were staying here? After we left Hong Kong for Hanoi, via several of his factories in Shenzhen, Yulin, and Nanning, the silences had lengthened. For hours he had been clearing his throat—and staring out of the window. Not once did he consult papers for the Vietnam meeting. Nor pore over Bloomberg's "Business Week" and "Market Snapshots."

He and I do not know one another well.

"Forget it," I said. "I'll buy some noodles."

There was a café over the road. It had westernized décor, and that probably meant clean and air-conditioned.

"You'll eat with your father," he shot back. His face was dark with heat. He glared—as though I had been responsible for this elongated road-trip.

On the remains of a sidewalk, Yuan held the car door open for my dad—who never hurried. After ten hours at the wheel, the man awaited instructions for the night's accommodation. Yuan looked miserable. I hopped out the other side—walked around the back and leaned in.

"Your servant needs to know where you want to sleep, *bàba,*" I told him. Yuan stood at my side, leaning against the open door. I envisaged a happier dinner with him.

There was little point resisting my dad's orders. Especially when his temper was brewing. This late summer tour of our family's inefficient, if lucrative, umbrella factories had unearthed a truckload of problems.

Besides, he paid my tuition in Canada.

"Is the restaurant air-conditioned?" I asked as he sent Yuan and the overnight bags to the Forbidden Palace Hotel—a dive of red pillars, even from this distance.

I was twenty-two. In a month, September 2005, I would return to studying corporate finance at the University of Toronto. (I had wanted to be a concert pianist.) During the previous four years, which included stretches at a private school in Oakville, Ontario, I spent more time out of China than in—with the occasional "holiday" to Beijing. Here or there, I felt like a confused visitor.

Except that this spring I made a friend. Emil is his name. He makes furniture. We met at an Apple store in Toronto's Eaton Centre where he was having trouble understanding gigabytes. He's very ignorant about computers—probably because he's Romanian-rural. I love him, I guess. We kid around.

"It'll have electric fans, Linn," my father said. Suddenly, he slapped my back. "Plenty of iced water to drink."

"Ouch."

He led the way, around the busy market corner. Before I knew it, the Hall of Eating Pleasure was in my face. At that moment, I should have realized what my dad had in mind.

The Hall was a popular, cramped and yet bare-looking eatery. No Caucasians in sight. At the entrance, its few flashing bulbs created an archway that opened onto half-a-dozen, green plastic tables, and twenty-four greener chairs—most of them occupied. With luck, there would be no space for either of us.

The yellow lanterns held no cheer. Street bedlam spilled into the room. Everyone was smoking. It was truly a bus depot of a venue.

"Do we have to?" I asked him.

He handed me a menu dotted with food stains, and we sat at a trestle near the kitchen. There's no way Ch'ien—that's his name—would patronize an establishment, or suffer a table, as crappy as this. I read the items on the list. I kept my head.

"How very quaint," he said. "They call it the 'Man Han Quan Manchu-Han Complete Banquet' and it's nothing of the kind."

"Let's leave."

Flipping the sticky pages, he muttered something I couldn't hear and took out an American cigarette. Clearly, I was not to select any dishes. I sat back.

"Live monkey brains?" I repeated, after he gave the order to our jug-eared waiter Fang. "Couldn't we avoid that?"

"Behave yourself, Linn," he said. "It's not McDonald's."

"Dunkin' Donuts is my hangout, actually."

"You'll love them."

I studied his face to get my bearings. He had that kindly tyrant look. Something he brought out at last-minute factory inspections when every smile from the workforce, from top manager to line operator, reflected unease, even terror, that he would cut wages or announce lay-offs. This hokey dinner was about money, too—"big picture" money. Because that's *bàba*. Gloves were coming off.

He knew how much I disliked the "exotic" extremes of Chinese cooking—of any cuisine, really. The feast was a shining example of Dad gone overboard: bear's-paw soup, an innocent monkey's conk. Do you laugh or cry?

"This is about Song Xi, isn't it?" I said, mustering my forces.

I know every ruse. His exquisite manners work well on underlings—but not on me. Dad is a schemer. More ruthless than Empress Cixi. He is nothing if not showy.

"It's about a meal on the way to Hanoi," he answered. Ch'ien looked injured. "Give some appreciation, please."

"You know I won't like brains," I said, wiping my forehead. "Seriously."

"You say that about a lot of things."

"Do I?"

"It's the idea of them that doesn't appeal, Linn. We're like that at first, with oysters or snails or raw scorpion."

"You're trying to toughen me up, again?"

"I'm feeding my son a few delicacies," he said. "Please, drink some water."

Song Xi was the twenty-year-old daughter of his best friend. I knew her in my brief spell at No. 4 High School in Beijing. She was clever, painfully shy, and wore Batman tortoiseshell glasses. I liked her well enough. She was now at Cambridge studying law.

Dad's idea was predictable. Dynastic, of course. He wanted the Hu only son to marry the Song only daughter.

In Hong Kong, the previous day, I refused.

Her father owned a wastepaper-packaging empire called Dragon's Teeth. He had become one of China's billionaires. I told my dad he should marry Song Xi himself. In U.S. dollars she was worth more than my independent-minded, rather stubborn mother (who was the bucks in our family)—and looked like a Taiwanese model.

He didn't find that funny.

To emphasize his claim that our Pingxiang stopover was not about Song Xi—and her clan's staggering net worth—he kept to the culinary arts at hand.

Somehow, the two of us grew accustomed to the Hall of Eating Pleasure and its bustle. I scoffed the bear soup, dumplings, a shark's fin, and shredded pork with chili and fish sauce. Fine flavours, every one. The steamed, jasmine rice was a whiff of heaven.

We did eat like emperors.

An hour, or more, passed.

He reminded me that an authentic "Man-Han Complete Banquet" was two hundred courses of the rarest kind and lasted three days. Rather like this journey from Hong Kong to Hanoi. A hefty period for me to keep talk of Song lineage off his lips.

Our waiter, the genial Fang, arrived at the table with a porcelain bowl and clean plates on a tray. At first I thought it was Peking duck lolling over the side.

You could tell—by his fading, comradely smile—that my dad was aghast at the presentation. I watched him like a Portia jumping spider.

Nonchalantly, but with evident pride, Fang manoeuvred the dish between a platter of roasted eggplant and some lotus root.

It was a monkey, the dimensions of a small cat. Its limbs bound with string, head resting on the bowl's rim.

"They intoxicate it with rice wine," my dad said. I could tell he was saying this to reassure himself. "Normally, you wouldn't get the entire body."

"Oh well," I replied cheerily. Getting on with these new ways.

My stomach was in my throat. As much because I didn't want Dad to sense fear in me, I could feel my chest rise and fall.

"Or if you do, it's fixed under the table with the scalp poking through a special hole."

"I see."

Solemnly, Fang arranged bowls of pickled ginger, fried peanuts, and herbs. I wondered if we should try to feed the monkey.

Fang bowed and left us.

My father stared at an open scalp, the ultimate Chinese buzz-cut still pink at its edges, where the knife had sliced.

I felt obligated to pip Dad to the post—and took up a spoon and scooped from the monkey's head. Sprinkling ginger and cilantro onto the white flesh, its veins still pulsing, I slipped the goodies into my mouth—chewed briefly and swallowed. Like a warm, aromatic custard, the brains tickled my throat.

As though seated with a Central Committee, my father savoured the performance for what I might disguise, and overcome.

Nonetheless, I reached for more rice and, with chopsticks, hooked a wad of string beans. He was not going to get the better of me. I sipped water, once, twice. At my turn, I scooped again, and with resolve, from the drunken monkey's cavity.

"*Yi xing bu xing*," Dad said, festively, darting a napkin to the corners of his mouth.

"Like nourishes like," I recited.

People, like Dad, use it to justify eating the weirdest shit. Tiger penises to cure impotence, bat's heart for blood circulation, cobra bile for indigestion, shark cartilage for cancer. You name it, the animal part feeds your part.

It's nonsense, of course.

"Song Xi's family is the sixth wealthiest in China," my dad told me. "Wealthier than your mother's."

"Bloomberg's Rich List?" I said. It was his little red book.

He poured more water into my glass.

"You can pretty much do what you wish, if you marry Xi," he said, finding it difficult to meet my eyes. "Play the piano?"

Dad is obsessed with rankings. He ranks my schools, international tennis players, MBA programs, investment houses—and, naturally, his factories and their employees.

"Not beforehand?" I said.

He ignored my question.

"Not work, if you choose, Linn."

Bàba laughed uneasily—as though inviting me to find merit in his suggestions. But I found in them disrespect. I did understand the importance of connections—*guanxi*—in China, or anywhere really, but Dad knew zip about me.

In our silence, he tapped the edge of the expiring chimp's plate and tried gamely to check out its eyes. Dad invited me to find this amusing.

Emboldened by his attitude, and the sight of the monkey, I decided to let Dad have it.

"Look," I said. "It's not just Song Xi I'm not marrying. I'm not ever marrying anyone."

He sighed—and swatted the notion aside.

"You'll change your mind," he said, opening a fortune cookie. The sort he never ate or read.

"No, *bàba*," I replied. "Not a chance."

"Why so adamant?"

Bloomberg had no category for my kind.

"If Song Xi is not the one, and you're being very stupid about her, I must say," he continued, "there will be others."

"There's no woman in my stars," I told him. "I'm not made that way."

He looked amused.

"Nothing good comes of free courtship, Linn," he sailed on. He thought I slept around. "I will get you a match to be proud of."

"Dad, I'm gay." I said. "You'll have to find me a man."

He nodded, strangely enough. "Drink your water." Carefully, he folded his napkin. He had the decency to take in what I'd told him—and simply gazed at me. I held his look.

"Marriage to Xi would be even easier, then." He glanced at the monkey. "Wouldn't it?"

"It would be more difficult."

He patted the napkin.

"Does your mother know?"

"She knows."

Dad smirked, as though he had lost a poker hand, and reached into a pocket for his wallet.

"It's not a phase," I said, trying to be helpful.

He waved Fang to our table.

"We'll talk another day, Linn."

"No, Dad," I said. "I've told you, and it's not easy to say it."

"Disgusting, Linn." He leafed through some bills and placed them on the table. "I will sever payments to you if you persist."

"Go ahead."

"You dare me?"

"You'll lose face."

"I'll lose it anyway."

We paused in our ping-pong.

"I'm discreet, Father."

"Are you, indeed?"

I closed my eyes and thought of Emil—who would be cheering. This talk with my father was a lot to absorb for Ch'ien and for me.

Old Fang held out the bill. My father waved it aside and indicated notes on the table. The two men exchanged pleasantries. Our ancient host, sensing an important figure in Ch'ien, went to fetch more tea and almond cakes to replace the torn-apart cookies.

Surveying the debris, we sat at the table like a pair of undertakers. The sozzled monkey was now quite deceased in its bowl—attended by wreaths of spilled rice and bean sprouts. I looked past the shutters and watched bicycles. Market gas lamps came on.

"You sent me to the West," I said eventually. "You might stand by the results."

"Ha," he replied. His cheeks were flushed. "You come back a troublemaker."

"I'm completely myself, Dad," I said. "I'm what you wanted."

Another cigarette. The clatter of the kitchen. I squirmed on my green plastic chair.

Forgetting the promised tea and pastries, my dad rose from the table and I followed.

"What did your mother say?"

He indicated the exit.

"About what?"

"Your disposition."

We walked toward the street. Old Fang, holding a teapot and plate, called to us—but my father marched on. I shrugged for the waiter's benefit.

"She told me not to tell you." It was my turn to sigh.

"Hmm," he said.

We headed in the direction of the Forbidden Palace Hotel.

"She's okay with it," I told him.

He chuckled. Dad crossed the busy street and I pursued, somewhat annoyed at such a race.

"*Yi xing bu xing*," I said, thinking of Emil and not the monkey.

"So," he replied—a worker's smile.

We reached our lodging. I followed him up the steps.

He never again mentioned Song Xi or the wastepaper-packaging dynasty. Not to me, anyway.

In September, he paid my fees.

You Turn Your Back

Mofo lives next door to Mrs. Shooter. He's big trouble, she knows that. Leather boy. Tinderbox. Mofo knifes bikers in his own chapter, beats heaven knows who. She keeps away from him—Brummie white trash. Like she did with her "Satan's Choice" husband and two sons. *Can't trust men worth a farthing*, she often says. Neighbours neither.

Mrs. Shooter first hears Mofo's words—and someone screaming back—as she walks, against the wind, to her gate. The terraced houses, and bungalows, stand on Culmington Grove. Hard and cracked the words are, like thunder on the Lickey Hills. Mofo is inside with peroxide-lady Agnes—a washed-out teenager, really. Pointy-faced, his guinea pig. Threatening words. For Agnes.

Then, quiet. Except for these westerlies.

Mrs. Shooter holds on to the gate. In a clattering, February gust, she feels like that man in the advertisement: in an armchair, hair and tie blasted back by the purple hurricane from his TV set. Wasn't that Mrs. Shooter? Forever in a pickle about what to do?

More raised voices—"Motherfucker!" A splintering of wood.

Steadying herself at the gate, she notices over the Lickeys—past the prefabs opposite and the car factory—racing winter clouds from the Bristol Channel and Severn Valley.

Let Mofo stop.

An inside door slams. *Agnes*, she says to herself, *hurry away while you can.* The girl's silence gnaws at the wind. Some of the gate has flaked off. Black and rust in the wool of Mrs. Shooter's mittens.

Hurry, hurry away.

She lets the gate swing and trips back to her house. Waltzes the metal dustbins—crash, bang, wallop—and stumbles, puffing her cheeks. She re-stacks old planks of wood, hurling them along the ginnel between their two homes. She grabs at a beer crate, full of Mofo's empties, and hurls it at his wall.

She leans against a drainpipe. *Can you hear, motherfucker?*

"Hey!" says Mofo. He lurches from their back door. "Mrs. S! How's it hangin', love? Makin' a bit of a stink, aren't ye?"

"What's happening in there, Mofo?"

"Now, Mrs. S. … Got my red wings, yesterday. Agnes tell you? Off for them black ones today."

She shifts to look past his leather shoulder. Mofo clips the door with his boot. Then locks it.

"Oh, ah," she says, thinking at first to delay him. Red wings? Mrs. Shooter knew about that from her sons and their clubhouse gang. Rite of passage. Cunnilingus on a menstruating woman: red wings. Witnessed by the bikers and their bitches.

"Our Agnes will tell you."

Did he force her to watch?

"Day like this …," he says. "You should be by the gas fire, not out buying your crossword books." Mofo swings onto his motorcycle.

The revving pinches at Mrs. Shooter's ear until she cringes.

"Ride for granny to the paper shop?" He swaggers the machine out to the road.

"Have you harmed her?"

"Keep your nose out, love," he says. "Black wings, today. Gotta go."

At the clubhouse, it was a black woman's turn. Mrs. Shooter knew about that, too—she'd once witnessed a scene. *What's happened to Agnes?*

"Life's a cunt, ain't it, Mrs. S?"

Mofo pats the Harley seat.

"Gave up on your kind years ago, sonny."

He scoffs and revs the engine some more. "That ain't so fockin' neighbourly, Mrs. S."

Mofo rides away. "Satan's Choice" on his jacket baring its angelic ass.

"Y'damned scum!" she yells. *Just like Gabby and my sons.*

Blue mittens clenched, Mrs. Shooter punches on Agnes's door. "Useless men," she says to herself. Tossers. Her stomach clenches. She bangs and bangs until, between the bashing, she can hear the girl.

"Open the bloody door, dear! It's me."

Mrs. Shooter tears off one of her mittens so that she can rap more sharply. Both hands now: one bare, the other blue. Smashing fists into her reflection. Pounding, pounding. Flecks of paint from the gate. She beats them—petal-black—into the glass. They tumble from her mouth, rat-a-tat.

There's Agnes. Crawling to the door.

"Shitehawks" was her word for Mofo and Agnes when, in January, the biker tenants moved in next door. Mrs. Shooter was smarting from an incident at the local church, St. Michael and All Angels, where the Boy Scouts Committee of Ladies—five women in their Sunday best—had insisted she brew tea (and not manage a stall) during the annual jumble sale. "You have a knack with loose leaves," said one of the more daisified fascinators. Mrs. Shooter knew the pecking order. Tea ranked with mopping. The vicar sided with the coats and hats, patted her shoulder and moved on.

The putdown was to do with her being a former char, part-time at Cadbury's and Boxfoldia, not to mention a made-redundant-Austin-worker's widow—*hoi polloi.* They were wives: to a plumber, building contractor, driving instructor, school-crossing attendant, and an electrician. Hardly *nouveau riche*, but a squeak above Austin and char for it to count. They had telephones in their homes—and donated money as well as time to Vicar. She cut up greeting cards with crimping scissors and turned them into gift tags. Worse, she was not a member of the parish "Regular Giving Plan." Ecclesiasticard, Mrs. Shooter called it. God's standing order keeping Michael and Angels aloft.

Toffee-noses, she reminded herself afterwards, on the path to Tessall Lane. *Fascinators and bloody Midlands.* Mrs. Shooter decided to walk in Daffodil Park.

Normally, she would have ignored a seventeen-year-old like Agnes sitting on a bench in tight-fitting clothes. "Draggle-tail," Mrs. Shooter would have thought. Brummie trollop looking for blokes—even in this weather. But to spite the Committee of Ladies, or because of them, and the wintry chill, she walked up to her new neighbour.

"Sent you to Coventry then, has he?"

"Eh?" said the girl. She didn't trouble to raise her eyes.

"Ignoring you is he, your bloke?"

"Oh, it's you," the girl said. "Coventry?"

"Sending someone to Coventry. It's an expression."

"I've been to Coventry."

Mrs. Shooter nodded. "It's not important, dear."

"Got bombed, didn't it? Coventry Cathedral."

"Yes, love. In the war. Did you see the famous sculpture?"

"Dunno."

Pig ignorance of the young.

"The archangel and the devil," Mrs. Shooter went on. She sat herself down. "It's outside. Very famous."

"The angel stomping on a nigger? I did see that."

"It's meant to be Satan, love." Mrs Shooter frowned. The girl was shivering. "Are you okay?"

"I've been up all night," she said. "You hear everything next door, don't you?"

A train left Longbridge station. The elderly woman felt a powerful urge to move on—but for some reason remained. Across the park, the River Rae smelled of oil, silt.

"You must hate us, Mrs. Shooter. We're always yellin'."

"Your house is made of wooden planks, you know. I can hear you *breathe*."

"I'm sorry."

Agnes seemed barely interested.

"Do you know why my house is brick and yours is wood?"

Agnes grumbled something, impatient.

"Guess," said Mrs. Shooter. She wondered why she bothered.

The train rattled toward Birmingham city centre.

"Ran out of brass?"

"Lord Austin made the workers' estate in 1900. Every block of wooden bungalows, Canadian pine, has a brick house between. See over there?" She pointed across the strip of river and railway.

Agnes shifted on the seat. "Three little pigs tell him?"

Mrs. Shooter smiled. "The brick is a firebreak, my kind of house." The two sat still.

"What were you doing last night, Mrs. Shooter?" Agnes said. "I saw your light on at four in the morning."

"Gift tags, love," she replied. "I make them for the church jumble sales. Silly bee that I am."

Neighbours in silence some more.

"I got screwed by eight fellas, Mrs. Shooter," said Agnes, beginning to cry. "I passed out at the fifth, I think. At their club."

Mrs. Shooter stared at the disappearing train.

"Mofo thinks he's God, you know," the girl said. "It gets out of hand."

Mrs. Shooter's mitten rested on Agnes's forearm, but awkwardly, as though ready for the off. By the track and mucky river—in a park where daffodils grow. Steel and dark water in the women's eyes.

"Mike will know what to do," said Agnes that same winter, one evening in Mrs. Shooter's sitting-room.

"Mike?"

"Mofo doesn't know about him," said the girl, almost vengefully. "You should meet him. He'll help us both."

Both? The elderly woman nodded. "Why not try and work it out with Mofo? He'll settle down once he finds work. Then he'll leave those stupid bikers. My sons Stan and Nick went through the same routine. Is Mofo seventeen like you?"

"Twenty-two."

Agnes slipped thread into a coloured square of Christmas card, neatly snipped by Mrs. Shooter. Agnes knotted the ends and packed two dozen tags into a freezer bag.

"Is Mike a secret boyfriend?"

"Not likely," said Agnes. "He gives me advice like you do. Mike's your splitting image."

"Spitting, Agnes. Spitting image."

"No gold thread in these?" said the girl. She fingered a pile of cards.

"Don't try puzzling those cards out. Typical of my sons. Nick sends them. Or Stan. The postmark is always London. They forget to sign."

"It's blank, front and back, too."

"Let's call it a snow-angel card, Agnes. You can't see anything on it. Gift tags need colour."

Ignoring Mrs. Shooter, she punched a hole in the snow angel, slipped gold into it, and raised the card.

"Nothing's clear, love. People won't know which side to write on."

Agnes raised another white square, admired it, and did not reply. Mrs. Shooter felt uneasy. She wanted to think of Agnes leading her kind of ordered, secure, tag-making life, but without the bitterness. The girl needed guidance. Crabby friendship was the best Mrs. Shooter could offer.

"They must treat you like a dog at that 'Satan' place, Agnes," she said later. "Gabby, my husband, and our sons, shouted and carried on. I was never a person to them. Took me most of my life to realize it."

"What did you do?"

"Told them they were on their own, love."

"You left."

"Oh no, Agnes," she said. "I stayed and got rid of them."

"I don't want to do that, Mrs. Shooter."

"Turn your back? No dear, I don't suppose you do. I'm not very proud of it. In fact, I've often had second thoughts. Gabby died a few years after my decision. Stan and Nick found labourers' work down south. I forced them. Maybe what I ever wanted was a break. Some praise and affection. I don't know. It's too late now."

"Mofo's weak really, Mrs. Shooter," she said, jabbing a hole in another piece of card. "He won't do anything to me, except yell."

"Weak ones need the most work, pet," she said. "Or they escalate, like my two boys did."

"Mike thinks I should leave Mofo."

"Is Mike a priest? I bet he's never been in a relationship. Stay with Mofo, dear. Don't make my kind of mistake—it gives you one hell of a lonely life. Save Mofo from himself. Get his yelling to turn into something kinder."

"It's the first time you and Mike have a different opinion on something," said Agnes.

"I should have a chat with this wee laddie Mike."

Mrs. Shooter smashes a broomstick into the glass of Agnes's kitchen door. Wisps of silver hair slip from their grips. She catches the sound of a man's voice—is the television on?—even before the rest of the pane crashes to the linoleum.

She reaches in and snatches the lock aside. *Bastard devil, Mofo!* Agnes has propped herself against the stove like a puppet exhausted by play. Her face, like her arms, is a strawberry porridge; her lower lip bleeds. Oh my God. Mrs. Shooter makes a dry, croaking sound. Muttering, comforting, she helps Agnes to the living-room sofa in front of the television.

"A glass of water," says the girl. "They're giving Mofo a rough time at the club."

Mrs. Shooter hurries to the kitchen. Over splinters of glass, she yanks one cupboard door after another, hunting for a cup—then freezes. The man's voice cannot be coming from the television. It is turned off.

A man is in the house?

She can see, down the hallway, Agnes lying on the settee. Like a fish, the girl is mouthing something in the direction of the television. Her lips are bathed in light as though the set were on. Suddenly the girl heaves.

Mrs. Shooter fills a teacup with water and rushes back to Agnes. The television is definitely off. Where is this brightness coming from?

"Here," she says, kneeling. Mrs. Shooter looks about nervously and wipes Agnes's mouth with her sleeve. "I'll call the ambulance."

Mrs. Shooter's legs are shaking. She cannot stand. *Up, you old warhorse*, she tells herself.

Agnes is losing consciousness.

"There's no phone," Agnes says. "Stay, please."

"Mike was right," replies Mrs. Shooter. "Mofo's a monster."

There is an odour in the room. An outdoor dampness. Gently, Mrs. Shooter tips the cup—its sheen—between Agnes's lips, shivers and once again tries to stand.

"Stay awake, Agnes," she says.

A chill creeps about the sofa. Stench from the River Rae, Mrs. Shooter thinks.

"I said you should work things out with him, Agnes. What a fool I am."

The wooden bungalows are draughty.

"I must hurry to the phone box on Culmington, dear."

"Tell Mike you were wrong," says Agnes. "Tell him." She glances at a spot behind the kneeling woman and faints away.

Mrs. Shooter can no more twist than fly. Suddenly, she feels a fingertip on her left shoulder. She flinches.

"Mofo?" she says. "Please, stop."

Mrs. Shooter leans forward to protect the girl. As she holds her, she realizes Agnes is dead.

With effort, Mrs. Shooter clambers to her feet and turns around. Nobody there.

She hurries, as best she can, to the kitchen door and out past the ginnel and its dustbin lids. No sign of Mofo nor a Mike.

"Tell Mike yourself"—what was Agnes talking about? Mrs. Shooter runs toward the Culmington phone booth. It stands there bright red, its tiny windows missing. Door off its hinges.

She gazes at blue wires where a handset once lay. The coin box is dented.

Mrs. Shooter bends over and rests her hands on her thighs. The cement floor smells of urine, nub ends.

"Angel," she says. "Angel."

Her disbelieving eyes in flames.

More Than Anyone on Earth

How far do I go, Zack? Scott was thinking of Zachary as he stepped onto the Algueña road from the three-o'-clock Alicante bus. La Canteriana, Spain, June 2001. The asphalt gave, like a sigh, beneath his runners. *How can anything survive here?* The summer heat was worse inland, more than ninety degrees. In the last town, Novelda, streets were deserted and shuttered for siesta, a plague of closed doors, as though no-one dared walk the ground.

Scott rifled in his shirt pocket for the farmhouse-on-a-hillside photograph Jacky had provided. There it was, just above him on the stony ridge, more goatherd's refuge than a farm. *Choice angle, Jacky*, he thought, comparing photo and tumbledown building. "*Mi casa es su casa.*" How alluring that sounded in Crooked Hollow, Canada.

He gazed at the vast, shimmering valley—a baked patchwork of almond groves. In the distance, row upon row of olive trees, parched soil. "When it comes down to it," Jacky had said in Ontario, slurring her words, "friends are what count." Beyond that, a sudden thrusting-up of rock—the famous Iberian quarry, source of Jacky's collection. A faceless, marble summit.

Scott swung the hockey bag over his shoulder and hiked along the track. Sky the bluest blue, ground an exhausted flesh colour: burnt ochre, dust. He cut across a field, his feet sinking here too. This time to the ankles. After a few deep strides he hopped and skipped to the path, leaving a galaxy of footprints. *Just three months shy of graduating, Zack. You didn't give any of us a chance to help.*

The earth was powder. How did the almonds, oranges, and olives survive? A breath of wind would lift the soil away. *I'm asking over and over. Two years later. Do friends count? Did I count for you, Zack, when you took that Wolfe Island ferry?*

Valley breezes across his face, Scott reached the farmhouse and stood by its well. Cicadas droned in the heat. Like majestic, dancing hands, the Sierra de Algayat mountains lay before him.

PICTURE POSTCARD—FRONT VIEW
(FAMOUS DORKS EDITION)

Couple in a restaurant.

CONCERNED MAN TO SLEEPING WOMAN: It's not you. It's just that I'm very talented. I have to have my space.

WOMAN: [snoring] Zzzz …

2. PRE-BOARDING

"Anyone home?" said Scott.

Peering through the first doorway, he rattled the beads that hung there. Inside a kitchen, he placed his luggage on the child-sized table.

Scott stared out of an open window that ran the length of a wall and whose massive shutter opened—awkwardly, surely?—across a faucet, crockery and pans on a draining board, and a stacked-up sink. The hazy valley beyond. Its lungs drew him in. Pressed away. The entire scene felt too near. *You could have spoken out, Zack. On that home stretch. Even Captain MacDonald warmed to you.* A line of ants ran along the floor and up to a bulging plastic bag—"Supermercado Continente"—hanging from a drawer handle. A torn package of biscuits lay on the stove, next to an over-ripe tomato.

Was Jacky expecting him?

Once more, he called her name.

To shut the window, he realized, you would also have to clear the counter of five or so magnums of Soberano brandy and an assortment of wine bottles. It must have been open a long time. *Big deal, so you were a fag and half Mohawk, Zack. Who the fuck cares, these days? Most didn't care. They knew. All of them. But you listened to the name callers and "wigwam fairy" shit. You needn't have done that. You'd have made a fine officer. That's what scared the bigots, and you.*

He looked at the sunny, struggling room and decided he would wait Jacky out: an earth floor and beamed ceiling, new cupboards, the low door leading to an inner courtyard. Scott heard a creak of bedsprings. Or was it the old refrigerator? He opened its door— three Schweppes tonics, a tin of sardines, and one beer. He found an opener amongst a package of candles on the stove.

The cicadas buzzed more insistently, drowning out even the jangling fridge. Scott realized he should never have come. It was Zack he was looking for, not Jacky. *I have to pretend, like the others, that you were unstable. When, in truth, you'd had enough of threats. That's it, isn't it?* A tremendous heat robbed this place of willpower—some essential human battle had been lost. There was only the waiting. Only the ants, flies, and whatever came in through the open window. Or door. Through a grove. *I should never have come.*

"No rental car, Scott?" said a voice from within the house. "How will we get around?"

PICTURE POSTCARD—REAR VIEW
(FAMOUS DORKS EDITION)

La Canteriana, Spain. June 2, 2001.

Hi Zack!

Cool card, huh? Arrived here ok, via New York and Barcelona. Jacky's introduced me to this zany 25-year-old from Manchester. Her name's Anna. She lives here part of the year, teaches English and paints landscapes. What a life! She's a real beauty, Zack. Is this it? Amor, at last. (Shannon will be furious). Haven't touched her yet, though.

Adiós for now,
Scott

P.S. Did you ever hear of Bloomsbury? It's British and could be marmalade. Check it out, please? I'm desperate. It's really important.

❖

3. DEPARTURES AND ARRIVALS

"Veronica Douglas is such a bore," said Jacky, forgiving Scott the rental car. She handed him a bowl of peaches. "But at least she owns a vehicle."

Jacky indicated some dilapidated lawn furniture—"my loggia"—next to a shrubbery squeezed behind a trellis.

"She thinks she's a famous artist. They call her '*Doña*' at the Canteriana bar. I'm surprised they haven't crowned her."

Scott tucked into a peach.

"Throw the quarry on the partridge," Jacky said. She tied a checkered scarf around her head. "Veronica will be expecting us."

"Do what?"

Jacky looked her guest up and down. "Toss the pit on this bush." She spoke slowly and raised her voice—as though interpreting.

Scott held up the remains of the peach and glanced at the shrubbery.

"Precisely, dear," Jacky said. "I forget you're Canadian."

He missed the shot.

With swimsuits in hand, Scott and Jacky climbed the hill on the other side of valley. Veronica's ancient farmhouse lay in the distance—Umbría de Algayat Alto. A sprawling terracotta building amongst acres of almonds and olives.

"She's the centre of the universe," Jacky said, "mainly because of the swimming pool. *Mucho ambiente.*"

Scott nodded. His flip-flops sprayed soil. "What's that mean?"

"A lot of atmosphere."

Jacky pointed across the field to an elderly man walking sedately with a long stick.

"Coo-ee! Coo-ee!" she said. "It's my goatherd."

The man walked on. Scott wondered whether he was quite out of earshot.

"Veronica's like Peggy Ashcroft, you know. A bit *Passage to India.* Hugely tedious. Her house is crammed to the rafters with collectors at present. There's a massive 'Antiques and Interiors' fair in Malaga. So of course they're here. Name-dropping pals from her London period. Every year, they come. She prefers Lord Toby and Sir Tits the best. That's Tristram's nickname: Tits. Don't tell him I told you."

Veronica's world sounded like the one Jacky tried to create on Quarry Falls Road in Canada: the British-in-Crooked-Hollow. Why had he not considered this? Was he so anxious to leave Southern Ontario? Loosen up, Scotty, he told himself.

"Ignore the fashion chatter," Jacky went on. "Drink the punch. They gab about William Morris wallpaper versus Colefax and Fowler. *World of Interiors* stuff. White mahogany, sisal rugs."

A herd of goats rounded the corner and wandered into a field alongside some Franco-era cave-houses. Followed by the shepherd.

"Coo-ee! Coo-ee!" Jacky said again.

At barely a hundred yards—the old fellow pretended not to see.

"Deaf as a post," Jacky said. She gesticulated wildly. "Those bloody goat bells. Clink clunk. It drives one potty."

The man hurried off.

"Drunk," she said, opening the gate. "Pity the poor goats."

PICTURE POSTCARD ——FRONT VIEW

(FAMOUS DORKS EDITION)

Sketch of two women on the town:

WHITE WOMAN TO BLACK WOMAN: Don't be silly. You'll be right at home. It's a very mixed bar.

TRANSLATION: 3 Latinas, 2 Afro-Americans, 646 white people.

4. BOARDING BY SEAT ROW

"They organize year-long for this, dear," said Jacky, a few days into Scott's visit. "The 'Moors and Christians' parade. Nuts about it, they are. *Everybody* joins in."

A horse and rider thundered back and forth in the centre of the road. Scott and Jacky found a spot along the cramped Novelda route.

"Aren't those your friends?" said Scott. He pointed to a group of sunburned British, dressed in white, jostling for position in front of a boarded-up video store.

Jacky waved—but they ignored her.

The horseback messenger, a grand vizier, crimson robe and silver piping, swerved before the spectators, repeating the manoeuvre a few doors down.

"But then it *is* Spain," Jacky said. "Celebrate everything. Southern Spain especially. You can't get the creatures to do hard work."

In the distance, drummers struck up a languid beat.

"I was rather hoping the sky would be more pink," she said, looking beyond the unlit electric lights draped above the street.

A phalanx of dark figures swayed towards them. "Moors are so chilling," she added. "No wonder the Christians threw them out."

You would have loved the Arab men, Zack.

"Pests," said Jacky, reaching for a handkerchief to wipe her brow and eyes.

PICTURE POSTCARD—FRONT VIEW
(FAMOUS DORKS EDITION)

WHITE WOMAN IN FRONT OF A WALL: Why can't they be made to speak English? I'm sure they're talking about me.

PICTURE POSTCARD—REAR VIEW
(FAMOUS DORKS EDITION)

La Canteriana, Spain. June 4, 2001.

Hi Zack:

We're scratching our heads. Jacky's disappeared. I bet it's my fault. I found some photographs. Twenty or more guys my age, taken outside at her well. Judging by the clothes, these shots go back years. Jacky's little fetish? I'm now officially part of a collection, I guess. As you would have been. When I asked her about it, she said, "Friends are friends, Scott. You mustn't pry." Next morning, the pictures were gone, along with Jacky. Manchester Annie says it's to do with the "Moors and Christians" festival in Novelda. The Brit. crowd told her they were going to Alicante for dinner and not to the parade. (Seems Jacky is unpopular hereabouts. "Takes advantage," Anna says. "Plus the booze problem.") We'll find her.

Adiós,
Scott

P.S. One of the Brits, Veronica Douglas the painter, gave me a book on the Bloomsbury Group. It's definitely not jam. Also, she told me that Jacky warned her to "lock up the silver" when I'm around!!! This Veronica Douglas is well-liked around here. I can see why.

5. FINAL BOARDING

Some of the men had blackened their eyes with kohl or painted them tawny red. Other Moors in the pageant—and a few were women—wore bold earrings, thorny-looking beards, and had stained their faces. Drummers marched, adorned in white djellabahs.

Should I leave you here, Zack?

As far as the eye could see, row upon row of advancing men— squeals of oboe, trumpet, amid the thundering bass, and snares. Ethiopian tribesmen, fiery plum-dark skin, precious stones in the soldiers' helmets and shields, the subtlest of embroidered silks.

Each company of eight was more imaginative, daring, than the next. Scabards shifting. Rif dancers to a bongo beat.

PICTURE POSTCARD—FRONT VIEW
(FAMOUS DORKS EDITION)

Sketch of two men in a gay bar.

WHITE MAN TO BLACK MAN: I'm not racist. In fact, I'm very turned on by black men.

PICTURE POSTCARD—REAR VIEW
(FAMOUS DORKS EDITION)

La Canteriana, Spain. June 5, 2001.

Hi Zack:

Anna and I are an item. The moon shines full over Novelda, I'm telling you! Can't believe my luck.

Anna says Jacky will return. She always gets temperamental around her men guests and the "Moors and Christians" parade. According to Anna, "boys" are never what Jacky really wants. "Round and round she goes," she says of Jacky. "Canada, England, Spain, Canada. She never stays anywhere more than a few months." I do now get the picture. Who would Jacky be if she stayed somewhere long enough? It seems her father had a hankering for younger men, too. "English disease," Anna calls it. What a shame for our Jacky. "She loved her father more than anyone on earth," Anna said.

Yours,
Scott

PICTURE POSTCARD—FRONT VIEW
(FAMOUS DORKS EDITION)

WHITE MAN READING A NEWSPAPER: Why are they always so angry?

6. CURRENCY EXCHANGE

"*Inglés?*" said a short woman next to Scott. She was engaged by Jacky's commentary on the "Moors and Christians" parade. "Are you English as well, young man?"

"*Canadiense,*" Jacky said. "Far away, *muy lejos.*" She indicated the Novelda main square—then, in a shooing motion, the hills.

Another row of men swept by, its leader striding from one side of the street to the other.

Evidently, Jacky felt that "*Canadiense*" and "Canada" required elaboration.

"Alicante?" Jacky said. She named the nearest city as though it were a perilous step on life's journey. She shooed and swept some more. "Then, A-t-l-a-n-t-i-c-o Ocean. *Comprende?*" Jacky leaned forward. She pointed in opposite directions at the same time.

The Moorish leader's goosesteps were long, painstaking—drowned out by the drums. Father of men, he courted the onlookers, come this way, admire my clothes, the line of my shield. Cower at my army, taste your fear.

"West, east," said Jacky, with a wink in Scott's direction. "Does it matter?"

Jacky nodded to the bemused woman. "C-a-n-a-d-a."

The Spaniard's eyes widened.

"The woman does understand English," Scott said.

"It's getting dark," replied Jacky, oblivious. "The lights should be on soon. Ignore Mrs. Dye Job. She'll be inviting you to visit the family next. Kids, grandchildren, aunts, uncles. Some six-hour repast with eternal friendship thrown it. Who has the time?"

"She does understand, Jacky."

"Oh, they always look as though they do."

Scott gazed at the unlit lightbulbs hanging over the street. Coloured figures swirled around the glass like miniature dervishes. In flight.

"*Su mama?*" said the Spanish woman to Scott. She spoke in a confidential way. Your mother?

"No," replied Scott. "A friend."

The woman, who smelled of lavender, muttered something.

Electric lights burst upon the procession.

"Never heard of Canada, most of them," shouted Jacky excitedly. "They think it's part of *Andalucía* or a suburb of Madrid."

Novelda cheered at the spectacle.

Scott stepped between Jacky and the woman. "This is when King Ferdinand and Queen Isabella turn up, right?" he said, peering into the distance.

"The Christians," she nodded, straightening her shoulders. "They'll be here imminently." Jacky resumed her watch over the Moorish men. "General Franco ran the trains on time."

PICTURE POSTCARD—REAR VIEW
(FAMOUS DORKS EDITION)

La Canteriana, Spain. June 12, 2001.

Last one, Zack:

I'm going to stop writing cards. It's like stashing everything away. Or stealing the silver! Let's just say I loved you, man, and I'm broken up that you've gone. I wish I'd seen that coming. I wish I'd understood you better. I've told Anna about us, my best friend ever. She and I will stay in Spain a month or two. Then a trip to Manchester. Wish me luck!

There is still no sign of Jacky. We found out she's visiting a young man, Thierry, in Alicante. "I'm thierribly sorry, Scott," says Anna, "but you've been usurped already." It seems Thierry has a battalion of queer friends who, according to Anna, will be lured to La Canteriana for a grand fiesta to celebrate Jacky's birthday this summer.

I kind of left you in that "Moors and Christians" parade, Zack, but with the Moors up front, real guys. I thought you'd approve. Don't worry about the Christians. They're always late, it seems.

Scott

PICTURE POSTCARD—FRONT VIEW

(FAMOUS DORKS EDITION)

WHITE WOMAN LOOKING DOWN FROM HER OFFICE WINDOW: What more do they want?

7. GATE CLOSING

Lights were strung in the shape of Moorish scimitars—an avenue of glittering half-moons. As far as Novelda's Casino Square.

"We're *turistas*," Jacky explained to the squat Spaniard. "Foreigners."

"Ya, ya," the woman replied. She looked flabbergasted.

The procession grew larger, filling the street with costume and noise. People wiped their faces and joked about the oppressive heat.

"Your accent's too difficult for her," said Scott to Jacky. "I can't make out the rest she's saying."

"Mine, dear?" asked Jacky. "I've been coming here for years. It's crystal clear."

The final Arab leader was an assassin, dressed in black and gold. The crowd roared at this marble-faced *übermensch*. Youngsters screamed his name, "*Moro, moro!*" Like a matador poised for the coup de grâce, he stalked the spectators—couldn't hear them.

Jacky sprang to her toes in delight.

"*Y su papá?*" the Spanish woman persisted with Scott—and smirked. And her father?

Jacky swung around.

"What's the woman saying?" said Scott.

"She thinks I'm like a little girl," Jacky replied.

The Spaniard chuckled—a worn joke. Flicker of gold between her lips.

"*Basta*," Jacky said. She leaned into the woman and drew a line across her throat. "Enough."

"The lady knows you, Jacky?"

"She thinks she does, Scott."

"Right."

"She asks where my father is!"

"*Pobre, pobre*," lamented the woman. She tugged on Scott's arm. "Poor thing."

Jacky sighed. "Who does she think she is?"

"How strange," said Scott.

"She an infant," the Spaniard confided, in English. "I hear them. *Señora* Jacky, her friends, every day in my grocery store in La Canteriana. I listen. Every day."

Jacky raised her hand as though taking the salute. "Please shut up, woman!"

"You recognize me, *Señora* Jacky, don't you?"

Jacky lowered her arm as though air required parting—and looked, in vain, for Ferdinand and Isabella who would soon rid Spain of Moorish pestilence.

"In La Canteriana, we know Jacky Dowling," the woman told Scott. "She lives on the moon."

"A perky person," he said.

Jacky glanced over her shoulder.

"Ya, ya, English people," replied the grocer. "Every day perky, *señor.*"

She spat into the gutter.

Primavera

per Rosa Regàs

I come as Hansel came on the moonlit stones
Retracing the path back, lifting the buttons.

—"The Underground" Seamus Heaney

It was Stephen's first massage. And on Galiano: heart, to him at least, of west-coast cool, nature trails, and trust fund hippies.

Thank Christ she's got the face of a frying pan, he thought, undressing. *Who needs a looker over you?* Sky Woodland is the masseuse's name. They must have smoked up at *her* christening. He peered through blinds at the faded sunflower mural on Mid-Island Grocery. A white-streaked longhair thumbed a ride out front. Stephen smiled—never very patient with "alternative." He'd grown up poor.

"Our daughter's getting married, Gracie," he said from Galiano that morning. "You sent her a garter and a set of what?"

"Garter's a wedding favour, Stephen," she replied, long-distance from a Toronto basement. "Tradition has it that wedding knives, two of them at least, are worn at the girdle."

"You didn't explain that to our daughter?"

"I did, Stephen. I did. Believe me. I told her that 'to wed' means to become mad. I looked it up for her: 'to be wild with anger or desire.'"

Stephen smoothed the paper surface of Sky Woodland's table—thought of a wedding sheet, shroud—and climbed aboard, face down. A few minutes later, Sky—as in Woodland—tapped on the door.

"You're a real peach, Gracie."

"I've got the dictionary right here, Stephen: 'To pawn or pledge oneself as hostage ...'"

"Leah's barely twenty, Gracie. Some mother you are."

"'Wedbedrip': 'to service a lord before reaping his corn!' It's dreadful. Dreadful, Stephen. Look at us."

"Did Leah say anything?"

"'You're full of shit, Mom,' is what she said."

"That's my girl. You told her the true reason you're not coming, Gracie?"

"'Weddying and hangying are destiny,' Stephen?"

"Will you put the damn book down, Gracie? It's your only daughter we're talking about here. Did you tell her the truth?"

Sky walked in. Stephen squirmed at the pleasure of lying naked on a table. Upon a crisp, white page.

"So, we're going to un-tense those muscles?" she said.

Sky arranged the sheet tidily.

"My daughter's getting married this afternoon," he replied.

"That so?" Her voice was raspy, cheerful. "Gotta get that body singing, right?"

"You give her away, Stephen. You're good at that binding-in-wedlock stuff. Life's little conventions."

"Little? She'll never forgive your absence, Gracie. I'm not sure I do."

"What the heck difference does it make?"

"It's ritual."

"Hers. Not mine. I gave her my blessing already."

"A wedding ceremony means something to her, Gracie."

"To her or to you, Stephen? Does it? She'll learn."

"Why not tell her the real reason, Gracie? That you're pissed off. Say it, Gracie. Aren't you? Are you too ashamed to admit that?"

"It was twelve years' work, Stephen. I have a right to be mad. I was in the violets under Mercury's right boot ..."

"What?"

"But that's not why I'm staying home."

Sky pressed a button on the tape machine.

"Neat," she said, for some reason. "Rest your head in there, Stephen. Forget everything. Listen to the forest."

Enviro-mood, he thought. How Galiano.

"Imagine wind in those redwoods, Stephen. A stream below."

This'll never work. His shoulders stiffened. *You never deserved us, Leah.* His stomach tightened. *Boy, oh boy. Either of us.*

"Gracie, okay. Grimaldi Press is a setback. Leah has to suffer for that? She'll be married much longer than your art books take."

"I won't be attending, Stephen. I can't now, anyway."

"They gave you another contract, Gracie. Come on."

"'Turn each section of Primavera *into four separate books?' I can't do it anymore, Stephen. I'm not Proust. Who gives a toss about the floor of some decrepit, fifteenth-century Italian oil painting? It's the second time Grimaldi's dissed me. I can't bear it."*

"You're studying the garden in the painting, Gracie. Not the ground. You're looking at a grove. It's wonderful."

"It's absurd, Stephen. Why don't you do it? I give up."

"What was left? People have studied the rest, honey: clothes, gestures. Everything. Provenance, date. Where Botticelli bought the paint, for fuck's sake."

"It's absurd. I'm a lunatic. Should never have started the project."

"Seashore through the clearing, Stephen. Hear the gulls? It's May. Think cornflower, daisies. That's it. Now focus on the blade of grass. Hear the word, 'spring.'"

Spring? We're in trouble, Sky Woodland. Let's change the channel. Spring?

"Relax, Stephen, Relax."

Spring?

"'Spring.' Try to focus on it, okay?"

Sky lifted the sheet from his back. Scent of patchouli as she walked by.

"Nobody wants my work. Twelve years, Stephen! Botticelli painted Primavera *for two teenaged orphans, Lorenzo de Pierfrancesco de'*

Medici and Semiramide Appiani who didn't want his ridiculous efforts, either, hanging over their bed. They didn't even want to get married."

"I know, I know, Gracie. We've been over this. You're going to hurt our daughter Leah. That's what this argument is about."

Sky lifted the stopper on a bottle and began rubbing her hands.

"Nobody wanted those Italian orphans in the 1400s, or in the painting. Married? Nobody cared."

Sandalwood in his nostrils.

Gracie began to cry.

"'Spring,' Stephen," said Sky. "The fern."

Sky stood over him. Amber oil trickled between his shoulder blades.

"'The depth of the drop,'" she said, "'is the height of the moon.'"

"You're a very selfish woman, Gracie. I want you to know that."

"Those city-state battles, children forced to marry. Cruel, evil, it was. Things don't change much, do they?"

"No-one's forcing Leah to marry, if that's what you mean."

"Leah's been corrupted, like every other young person."

Sky's hands swept down around his neck, along the spine down to the crack of his bum.

"You're such a screw-up, Gracie."

"The bride, Semiramide, was shell-shocked at marrying at all. God knows how old she was. Eleven? Thirteen? Lorenzo had his head in the clouds every minute and was probably queer."

Over his buttocks.

"How can you do this to Leah?"

"From you, that's ripe, Sir Gadabout. What of your girlfriend Marnie Farber? You were both in Europe again weren't you, Stephen? Six months, was it?"

Like a genie, Sky plunged over Stephen's shoulders. He groaned.

"Four months. Alone. Working. I've never abandoned Leah. Or you."

Through the creaking table, forest limbs.

"That right, Stephen? Leah doesn't see it that way."

  Gracie blew her nose.

  "You're something else, Gracie. You know that?"

  "Marriage makes everything worse, Stephen. Everything."

  "I'll pass it on," he said. "Leah was right about one thing, honey."

  "Yes?"

  "Your shit."

  "Go give our daughter away, Stephen."

  "We're finished, Gracie. You're ten years older than me and still you don't get it, do you?"

  "Want to end it again do you, Stephen? Did it ever start? Fine. So do I. Gig over."

He wasn't sure who hung up first.

"'Spring,' Stephen," Sky said. "Crocuses, hyacinths, snowdrops."

He gasped into primeval shadow. Ground his teeth. *To hell with it.*

I

TORONTO (EARLY JULY, 1985)

Gracie sing-songing in the kitchen doorway of their Annex house, butt-naked, skinny.

"Stephen, there you are."

She was always like this when her manuscript was going well. Hair-triggered. Insatiable.

"Very tempting." He returned the wiggle. "No time."

Redwater Meat Packers was on his mind—and a nineteenth-century painter, Rosa Bonheur, the subject of his latest film.

Hand like a stop sign, "I'm out of the door, Gracie."

She pirouetted for him. "Rosa Bonheur calling is she, Stephen?" Gracie stroked her hips, crotch. "Quickie?"

He marched over and pecked her breasts. Geranium pots, she called them.

"Pass me the phone directory will you, Gracie? I've lost their number again."

He smoothed the hair between her legs, caressed her nipples. "You're such a turn-off, Stephen."

He loved Gracie. Adored her. They'd have another kid. Move into a house. Only thirty-nine, she'd have tenure at the university.

"Where are we?" he said, fumbling the pages. "Redneck, Redoble, Redwater: St. Clair at Wychwood. Around the corner, really."

Redwater.

It was an odd name for a meat-processing plant, thought Stephen. Belly-slit calves.

He rested his hand on the 1985 Yellow Pages.

Suddenly, he imagined hoisted rib-cages. They rose from his mug of coffee. Gristle.

He caught his breath and dialed the Redwater abattoir.

Blood in the drains. Mooing. Why was he doing this? Death moos. Hustle, hustle. Body parts aloft. Couldn't he produce a blockbuster instead? Break records? Gracie was a start. That'd do for now. He'd celebrate her.

"I'm horny," said Gracie.

Her books dazzled the art world. She mooed primordially at his back. Stephen giggled. *Botticelli's Primavera: il faut cultiver le jardin* would be her third masterpiece: meticulously researched, controversial yet balanced, cautious—like her life. Pushing edges.

"Hands off, Gracie."

He turned his back, felt her against him.

With piss bombs and acid, "everyone in art history" was waiting for Gracie's publication, she told him. More interviews, tours, and a launch. She was well known. The competition desperate.

Gracie's hand unzipped his fly and slipped away the boxers.

"Gracie."

The publisher, Grimaldi, had contracted her for a book about flowers in the celebrated painting. Solely the flowers.

"Gracie, it's ringing."

People barely notice the forget-me-nots and poppies throughout the canvas. Roses, periwinkle. Here was Gracie identifying every strain and variety of flora, weighing a dot of a linen plant's role in the Main Picture.

"I dare you," he said. "I just dare you."

At the other end, Redwater picked up.

Stephen imagined disassembly lines and athletic figures in rubber aprons. Cows on ramps, pushed into pens.

"Public Relations, please," he said.

Captain Haddock hats yelling at one another. Pigs squealing.

"You don't?"

Black, shiny hands and electric prods.

"But we spoke yesterday … My company, Film Scene, is making a movie about unusual female painters … Rosa Bonheur is the current one. Heroic, brilliant woman. I'm fascinated by her. This is the producer, Stephen Goldmann."

Lost sheep. Hoses watering people down. Dung and fright.

"Well, who do you think would?"

Knives up and along.

Stephen imagined Rosa went through this with abattoir appoint-ments. Hustle, hustle. In George Sand's Paris, 1850s?

"I can bring proof," Stephen told the woman in Livestock Receiv-ing. "A press card from Film Scene. Will that do? Actually, I'm a serial bovine killer. APB material. 'Movie hack?' You said it. One o' those shady producer types."

Gracie took him in her mouth.

"Right. I guess slaughtering has changed in a hundred and fifty years."

Stephen raised an eyebrow.

Rosa Bonheur had spunk.

"No. Just for background. Twenty minutes. I've never been inside one, see?"

What did Rosa do in France—1853? No phone.

"I won't ask any questions, okay?"

Dressed in men's clothes to get inside the Roule abattoir to sketch. Anatomy.

"Promise."

Wore men's get-ups throughout her life after that. The Prefect of Police approved.

"No, I haven't."

Gracie's mouth bumped at his groin. She pressed him backwards over the table. He smelled her fragrant hair.

"Horses, bulls. That kind of thing. Some watercolours," he said, lying back. "Oils, mainly."

Rosa was once arrested by a gendarme.

Gracie clambered over him, one foot on the window sill, easing aside some carnations in a Pellegrino bottle—steering his cock.

"Bugger," she said, squatting on it. Urgent. "Oops-a-daisy, there we go."

Stephen heard clanking sounds at Redwater—old machinery. "You must get every sort, right? Minus a few buttons?" he said to the woman at the other end. "No, I'm a regular guy. Very sane."

Up and down went Gracie, Nokia slipping at his ear like stop-watch hands.

"Bonheur painted the finished versions, in fact … yeah."

"Ooh," from Gracie.

Paris cops charged her once—for being a man masquerading as a woman.

"What do you mean, 'Sides' …? Chops? Oh I see. Does she paint cutlets? Oh no."

Gracie nearly lost him, then slammed down. Her face flushed, she pressed a thumb into his thigh—again.

Gunshots at the slaughterhouse?

"No. The complete animal. Bonheur painted every bit. Yeah. No steaks. Entire body. Intact ... right."

Stephen wondered how come the woman at Livestock Receiving was so fascinated by this artist crap.

"Chewing the cud, drinking from the river in a rolling pasture," he said. "You know how they do. In context."

Was she chatting him up? Beef greeter was chatting him up.

"Oh baby."

What else to get a film crew into an abattoir? Welcome to the movies.

Gracie stirred around.

"The guts were homework," he told the Redwater woman quickly. "Bonheur always started with insides."

The livestock receiver confirmed a time.

Stephen was nearly there.

"Looking forward to it ... Pardon? 'Rachel Farber' did you say?"

Stephen slapped at Gracie's buttock—once, twice—jostled it like a jelly, pressed it open, closed.

"Rachel? Okay. I'm Stephen Goldmann. Did I say that?"

He was going to come. His balls flicked at the table edge.

He was coming.

"I'm sure you do. No. Ready for the Film Festival. Rachel, I …"

After the Franco-German war of 1870 and the siege of Paris, Rosa always wore a long black coat—"better go"—*with black frogs opening on a black waistcoat.*

"I'd better hang up, Rachel. Excuse … me?"

Stephen was coming fast.

Gracie snatched the phone away—*a man's white collar and cuffs, and a black shirt.*

"Oh yeah." He tossed the receiver away. "Yeah, baby."

After the war, Rosa kept her hank of hair short and brushed back.

"Oh no." The phone hit the window and bounced off. "Yeah."

Stephen's head backed against the toaster.

Gracie gripped the table, her knuckles pink and white beside his thighs.

"Bloody hell!"

The receiver landed in a wicker sewing basket.

"We close for lunch, Mr. Goldmann, by the way," it said distantly.

"Oh Stephen!"

"Mr. Goldmann?"

"I shall try to do better next time," Rosa Bonheur told the King of France on being awarded the nation's highest medal by the Paris Salon.

"Oh fuck, baby! Oh fuck."

"But I'll be out on the receiving dock," it went on amidst the coloured cottons and pins.

"Oh, Stephen!"

"Rachel's the name. Rachel Farber. You can't miss me."

The table legs screeched—convulsed.

"Oh, my fucking God!"

Dial tone.

Gracie let him pull out. He wrenched at his penis, gasping, wild. "Jesus."

Glistening, spent. He lay motionless, breathing fast. "Fuck."

After the war, Rosa painted tigers, lions, and the odd panther.

"You're incredible, Gracie."

Never looked back.

"Petals everywhere." Gracie dabbed his chest.

No more pastoral scenes for Rosa. Like she said: before taking up your brushes, be certain of your pencil.

Gracie had left the room, of course. Always did. Either that, or frenzied towel-wiping.

"Was it good for you?" Stephen asked himself out loud. He sat up unsteadily, pulled a paper napkin from under the breakfast plates.

"Speechless, Stephen. I am. Truly," he said.

Is that it, ma'am? That it, Rosa?

Gracie sang "Jerusalem" in the shower.

He tried to laugh. *At thirty, I want to be a girl like her*, he thought. "Among those dark sa-ta-nic mills." *Cool on the kitchen table. Missing every point.*

CALEDON HILLS, ONTARIO (LATE JULY, 1985)

"I used scissors," Rosa Bonheur said.

I don't like the word "handsome," but that's what you were, Hermana. Handsome woman. Hermana Farber—"Marnie." You still are, Marnie. Like your daughter Rachel of Redwater.

"What amused me was to cut out subjects," Rosa told her enquirers.

When I catch eye of you Marnie, that is. Swept-up red hair. Out there in the Caledon Hills designing kayaks.

Your slender face. Tiny, cup-handle ears.

Rosa refused to read, had so much difficulty learning.

You didn't like it when Rachel brought me home from the Redwater abattoir, did you Marnie?

Okay, I got my Rosa Bonheur movie figured out, at least in my mind—and couldn't stop thinking about it, and Rosa's unusual techniques.

Your show-jumping horses, and the paintings, were an excuse to visit the Caledon farm.

But I heard you, Marnie.

"Bit old for you, isn't he? The movie producer?" you said, thinking I was still outside with those horses: Mestral and Levant. Tying-up body cloths.

"I covered the white walls as high as I could with my shapeless sketches," Rosa said.

You didn't believe Rachel; she didn't believe herself.

Snip-snip.

You were courteous enough, Marnie.

"To begin with I made long ribbons," Rosa said, *"then I used to cut out, first a Shepherd."* Snip. *"Then a dog, then a calf."*

Your daughter was no bullshitter.

Snip-snip.

There they were, stunning "Rosa Bonheur" forgeries on the Farber wall: "The Horse Fair," "Cow and Bull of Auvergne," "Sheep," "Study of a Dog." Above trophies and rosettes of every kind. Rosa Bonheurs hanging in a sitting room west of Toronto. I couldn't believe my eyes.

Rachel giggled.

"Then a sheep, a tree." Snip-snip. *"Invariably in the same order."*

Rachel pointed to the Royal Agricultural photographs. My face felt clammy. "That's my father. He died of cancer," she said.

Snip-snip. Snip-snip.

"I'm sorry, Rachel."

"We're over that now, aren't we, Mom?"

You raised your head—and I could see the answer was "no."

"Two years, next month," said Rachel.

I looked at you straight, Marnie. My throat felt dry.

"I spent many days over this pastime," Rosa said. 1820s, wars raging beyond the shutters. Snip-snip, snip-snip. King Louis-Phillip ill-placed.

"Why don't you fix your guest a drink, Rachel?"

You seemed relieved, if apprehensive, that I'd caught on.

Rachel hesitated. "There's a new bottle in my truck," she said.

"Whisky is okay, Mr. Goldmann?" you asked.

I nodded and took a seat. "Call me Stephen, please."

"Coming up, Stephen!"

You grinned, once she'd gone.

"Rachel does this a lot?" I said.

"Bless the sweet girl," you replied, your banjo eyes sparkling.

"What do I do about her? She means well enough. She doesn't want to see me lonely."

Rosa's grandmother told her mother, "You think you have a daughter. You are mistaken."

"You're not looking for a husband, then, Marnie?"

"Hell, no."

"I was beginning to think 'Stud Farm,'" I said.

How we laughed.

"Wheel 'em in from downtown. Wheel 'em out," you said, dashing something away from your face. "Kinda looks like that, doesn't it, Stephen? I do apologize. I wish Rachel wouldn't do it."

"Wrong, wrong. She is a boy in petticoats."

"I'm not complaining. An hour at Redwater Packers was enough, to be honest. I needed to get out."

"Rachel loves animals. I can't think why she works there."

Snip-snip. Snip-snip. "A little hussar."

I looked across at the paintings and a design table ten feet long: end elevations upside down, Indian ink, body plans, compass, magazine cuttings, rulers.

"She didn't buy the Bonheurs to lure me and my movie, then?"

You snorted. "No-one's that important," you said. Charts and catalogues under the table. "Rachel may be twenty. But she's not too foxy."

Not she, Marnie.

You invited me to supper. Your uncertain, welcoming voice.

"We have a seven-year-old daughter," I told you. "Leah. Then there's Gracie to feed, bathe, and read to."

"Gracie?" you said.

"My wife."

You gazed at me. "Feed and bathe?"

"Gracie's writing a book at present."

You seemed impressed.

"She asks me to read her day's draft out loud in bed."

You smiled. Watching, watching. I couldn't believe my feelings.

You invited me for supper, Marnie—every bone in my body said yes. Eat. My heart thrummed.

"Some other time, then, Stephen."

You spoke it honestly. I believed you.

"Here's Mother's card," said Rachel. She clutched a drink to her young chest.

Did I want to leave?

"What's the book?"

"Spare me, guys," I said. "My wife's working her way from the right side of a famous painting, *Primavera*, to the left. With her nose down a daffodil, and her tush in an orange plantation. She'll take years, day and night, to complete it. Fall asleep in her seminars. Students'll hate her."

"You're not celebrating?" you asked.

"Try living with *Prima-frigging-vera.*"

The three of us strolled to Rachel's truck.

"Hold on." My hand rested on the hood. "How about I change my mind?"

You and Rachel glanced at one another.

"If that's okay." It didn't look as though it was. "Let me call Gracie. Her day with the blue wind-rapist Zephyrus, I can do without. I'll get enough of that story over the weekend."

Rachel rubbed her hands, looking at you. "There's a phone in the hallway, Stephen."

Wouldn't I love a daughter like that?

"Come on," you said. "I'll show you Rachel's ponies. Champions, the three of them. Eighteen hands."

We toured the stable.

"Gracie?" That was just what my wife needed.

"I'm under the arch of Chloris's right foot," she told me. "Bachelor's buttons, girl's lantern. Do you think I should do the weeds Zephyrus's knocking out of her mouth?"

"Could you feed Leah?" I said, raising my voice above the static.

"Chloris *is* splitting into Flora. No. I guess I should stick to the ground flowers," she said. "But what's coming out of her mouth is so … eloquent. Strawberry plants, I think. Maybe I can twist the rules a shadow of a shade?"

"Supper, Gracie? For Leah?"

"Who?"

I hung up.

"Marnie, I've changed my mind again. I'm sorry. Leah will never forget we missed her meal."

You must have wondered about me, Marnie.

"Your wife won't feed her?" you said.

"She's manic and stubborn and numerous other things I can't think of right now."

Or maybe *I* was.

You drove me back.

At the end of the road, I kissed you like I'd never kissed anyone. You tasted of sweet tea, Marnie. I couldn't stop.

Did I know how I felt?

It was July, 1985. I was twenty-eight. Seven years into the marriage. A beautiful daughter—Leah. I was stepping aside. "Shadow of a shade."

That was it.

I guess it was a beginning with you too. Or an end. I never really worked that out.

II

PARIS INTERLUDE (OCTOBER 1989)

What a joke.

"*Si'il vous plaît, madame.*" I called it out as plainly as I could. I'd been in the Louvre seven hours trying to forget you. "*Monsieur, je ne peux pas sortir.* Do you speak English?" An hour or so in one of its many washrooms-for-all, I rattled the lock. Jammed the lock down, to the side. Pushed and pulled. I couldn't believe it. No way would it budge. Damn the French. I was trapped in a lavatory. My mind raced.

"You're turning into your wife," you said, five years later, Marnie. "Buried in paintings and artists."

It was our last night in Paris.

"She's buried in one painting. Just the one, Marnie."

Gusty, raw October. I'd be staying on in Paris. Drizzle. The shedding leaves breathed life into us. I tied your hands behind your back. Rode you like a steeplechaser, first night at the Hotel Atlantis. "Go on, go on," you said. As if I'd ever stop. The Film Scene assignments were adventures and kept coming. A Canadian federal agency made me "Producer of the Year." I'd been in Europe since September, spent the final two weeks of it with Gracie in the Mediterranean; I wanted to tell you what had happened. I hadn't seen you for months.

You were a flâneuse, black-and-white movies, Food Lover's Guide to Paris. I inhaled your body. Craved it like someone possessed. Your breasts, your unravelled hair. I sucked on your freckled belly, the silky wetness of your ass, your nipples.

With your scent on my fingers, I worked on the set noon and night—burrowing into Francisco Goya. Eight weeks past a deadline.

You tasted of apricots and coffee grounds. I ate and ate. Spat your hair from my mouth. Held your blushing curls high. What had happened with Gracie in Spain—I hadn't the guts to say.

"Pouvez-vous m'aider? Mademoiselle? Help, please. Stupide moi." It wouldn't have happened in a men-only restroom. Would it? "Pardonnez-moi? Hey!" I poked my face—just—under the door. A pair of teenaged girls tittered and ran out. What were they saying? I thought of Eustace Le Sueur's painting Terpsichore— it'd captivated me before the bladder took over. That and the Redwater abattoir back home, haunting me still: firing squads of one; animals penned in. How could Rosa Bonheur sketch in a slaughterhouse? Amidst that? But Le Sueur. Back to Le Sueur. Why is this artist in my toilet trap?

You liked my fingers in your bum, Marnie—one, two, three. High fives. You writhed, in bliss, for the world.

SAILING WITH GRACIE AND THE EAST SPAIN PILOT
(SEPTEMBER 1989)

Gracie was upset. Grimaldi Press had panned the first half of her book—it's 1989, five years' work—from the wind-rapist to most of Venus. They wanted it rewritten.

On a rented yacht, we sailed from Marseilles the last fortnight of September bound for Formentera, one of the Spanish Balearic Islands. The first night—Golfe du Lion somewhere—she'd gone into raptures about the stars. She talked for hours about heavenly bodies, the sun, moon, and five old planets of the "astro-alchemists."

"Seven bodies celestial, Stephen. Don't you know anything?"

She went on and on. How they were related to ancient metals, the seven bodies terrestrial. Everything from her *Botticelli's Primavera,* of course.

Then she started weeping. I couldn't get her to stop. She wept for hours. On the deck.

PARIS INTERLUDE
(OCTOBER 1989)

You liked pain, you said, Marnie. Further. Go further, Stephen. Your eyes in the twilight—cress flowers—sparkling.

I stood on my tiptoes. Peeped through the crack in the door. One man after another glanced from the hand-basin mirrors. I know why Le Sueur's *Terpsichore* bothered me—apart from the fact I couldn't pronounce the title. Here was a fetching, country landscape, a young seventeenth-century woman at her leisure. Rustic, carefree … But now … Could I clamber over the top? No. It was so high. I'd have to fall over a seven-foot door. Cut myself in half in the process. I'm only five feet ten. No.

You licked at me, Marnie. Licked, and I couldn't reach. Do it man, you said. Do it. Your face hot and wet. My fingers turned.

SAILING WITH GRACIE AND THE EAST SPAIN PILOT
(SEPTEMBER 1989)

So Gracie trashed the Grimaldi publishers. A giant leap for her. She was going to finish the manuscript without them—and find a new publisher in the spring.

I knew she was petrified by what she'd done.

In her basement study, she'd upped and abandoned the flowers Venus walked upon, the ground that Cupid flew across.

"Bugger Botticelli."

Gracie never worked like this before. Without a publisher's welcome hand in sight.

She'd given herself ten days to recharge, fixating on the heavens.

PARIS INTERLUDE (OCTOBER 1989)

Punch me up, Stephen, you said. Arched your back and cried out.
Opened your lips wide. Starwort in the sun.
  My hand slipped through.

To one baroque-looking, fortyish Parisian, I said, *"Monsieur? La*
porte de ma toilette …" My hand high over the door. He shooed
me away. Superannuated Alice Cooper.

That seventeenth-century woman of Le Sueur's, amidst the pas-
toral-scenery-to-die-for, is playing a triangle. A metal triangle! Even
the sight of it is jarring. High-pitched ting-a-ling. Dance rhythm.

"*Excusez-moi!*" I said.

A middle-aged, well-dressed woman, a mother and daughter.
Yes, yes, they nodded, smirking politely. Saying nothing.

Ting-a-ling. Ting-a-ling.

They'd seen every trick. This was Paris. I could think only of
alarms. Maybe that's why it came to me then. Ringing. In an
idyll! If only the mother and daughter had smiled, not smirked.

"I can't get out," I yelled, exasperated. Xenophobes. "*Com-*
prenez-vous mon predicament?"

Ting-a-ling.

Who did they think I was?

I can't be here forever.

I untied you before you came. You grabbed for my chest. Slid your hands
over my stomach and thighs. Your smooth, unsteady, comely hands.
You loved me, you loved me, Marnie. I told you back. Cupped you.

SAILING WITH GRACIE AND THE EAST SPAIN PILOT
(SEPTEMBER 1989)

Everything I did, Gracie told me after a day at sea, was careless, wishy-washy—"and on board ship that's criminal, Stephen."

I'd joined an underclass. I ignored her.

As we sailed past the Pyrenees, we weren't talking. Mutiny on "Le Bleu," hired yacht of choice, its carved figurehead leading the way—no crew. I took out a sketchbook and roughed-in the Catalan coastline she was hugging.

The wind was rising. In the early evening, the sky turned ink-black, the sea choppy.

"Hands on deck!" said Gracie.

She studied the clouds.

PARIS INTERLUDE
(OCTOBER 1989)

You flowed like the storm outside. Over and over. Salty sweetness in our faces. Your voice rushing water. We were ourselves away. Leaves stuck on our balcony window. Hotel Atlantis—Saint Germain des Prés. Your red hair between my legs.

"You're turning into your wife," you said again, afterwards, at Le Boeuf Sur Le Toit on Rue du Colisée.

"Turning against her," I told you in the frenzied brasserie. Cutlery, plates, and crystal. Talk, talk. Sea urchins and venison before us. The first night—Art Deco, tiled floors—of recounting our lives.

Your bare shoulders.

GALIANO ISLAND, BRITISH COLUMBIA

(EARLY MAY 1997)

"Lay the flower aside, Stephen. That's it. Good," said Sky. In the bloodwarm darkness. Bones humming under her hands. "Forget the blade of grass. 'When you imagine spring, don't imagine willows, plums, peaches, or apricots. Just imagine spring.' Let the flowers go, Stephen."

Take the whole meadow, lady, he thought.

"'To imagine willows, plums, peaches, or apricots is to imagine willows, plums, peaches, or apricots. It's not yet imagining spring.' Let them go, Stephen. Hear the trail they leave?"

Is Sky for real?

"Feel their touch leaving you. Stephen." His shoulders tensed slightly. "Follow. Now, *follow*."

PARIS INTERLUDE

(OCTOBER 1989)

Someone entered the stall next to mine.

"*Un moment*," I said.

Whoever it was went very quiet. I bent down to see. A man. He tapped his foot.

"*Parlez-vous anglais?*" I tried to make my feet do a Charlie Chaplin I-give-up *V* sign. Leather scissor-wipes. Quite funny, I thought—dancing shoes.

"I've made a new friend, Stephen," you said. "Lewis. He designed a catalogue for my kayaks. Pretty talented fella. Guess what?"

I didn't want this.

"You screwed him?"

"You live in paintings and movies too much, Stephen."

"Life's not merely seduction and fucking, Marnie? What's with Lewis? Pretty or talented?"

"I told you, Stephen."

"Or is he more your age?"

"He's not my lover," you said.

Lewis-who-was-not-your-lover in Toronto?

Under the chandeliers and soaring ferns we stared at each other. Marnie, no. Please.

SAILING WITH GRACIE AND THE EAST SPAIN PILOT
(SEPTEMBER 1989)

We were in for a storm but I felt safe enough, so close to shore. Still, I decided to co-operate with the admiral—and made her a brandy.

"Bring down the mainsails?" I said, pouring myself gin.

The wind began to howl.

"We'll use the engine," she replied.

"Right," I said, wriggling my drink into its holder.

Gracie scoffed.

"You've had yacht training, Gracie," I said, tugging at the line self-consciously. "Olive Oyl detests Popeye's management style, okay," I said.

The sea swell grew.

PARIS INTERLUDE (OCTOBER 1989)

A hand appeared beneath the metal wall, fingers beckoning
lasciviously.

"I've got a Goya movie confirmed," I said at last. "In Madrid."

*Actually, I hadn't quite. I was still trying to understand what
had happened with Gracie. Goya's faces in an elbow, eyes in a finger.
Extra limbs and hazy sutures.*

"Tell me about Lewis," I said.

You looked askance, Marnie.

"You tell me about Francisco Goya," you replied.

*I knew you'd betrayed me. We sat and stared—at the Le Boeuf
Sur Le Toit.*

The arm came further under, cuff-links undone—pearl. I stepped
on the arm. Decisively. Gucci semaphore sabotaged.

Like a behemoth, I raged at the door. Colt's feet, kicking.
Anemone in retreat. Yelling. Sunflower at night.

Let me out!

SAILING WITH GRACIE AND THE EAST SPAIN PILOT
(SEPTEMBER 1989)

I turned on the navigation lights. Just a few miles from Cadaqués.

"'An anchorage, not a port,' it says here," I said, waving the
East Spain Pilot.

I gripped the cabin door. Pitch dark beyond. Rain, spray, at our cheeks. The sea rose higher, tossing "Le Bleu" like a cork. We struggled into our rain gear, eyes stinging, seawater at our ankles.

"We'll take it," Gracie said.

"Turn right at the light. There'll be a gap in the coast," I replied, trying to be jolly.

"Read the map, Stephen. The map. We've passed Cap de Creus." Gracie jabbed a finger at the plastic folder.

"'Easternmost point in Spain,'" I read out loud. "'Costa Brava: savage, wild, rugged.' Do we need this book?"

I clenched a rail, struggling with the chart in my free hand.

"The numbers, Stephen."

"Okay, okay. Look for Far de Cala Nans. A lighthouse. It's on a point," I shouted.

Gracie cursed. "They usually are."

PARIS INTERLUDE

(OCTOBER 1989)

Ambisexual toilets are not a good idea, are they? The name's too suggestive—even in the Palais du Louvre. Who can relax?

"I guess I'm sad about leaving," you said.

We'd been playing these scenes for years. Wasn't it erotic to turn away so often?

"Give me your hand, Marnie. Open your fingers."

"Stephen, what is it?"

I deposited a key.

"To my house."

"What happened? What happened to Gracie?" you said.

I can't cope with someone sitting next to me in the can. If we can't divide the W.C.s by age or orientation, let's stay with gender. It cuts down the neighbourliness.

SAILING WITH GRACIE AND THE EAST SPAIN PILOT (SEPTEMBER 1989)

"Do you want this information or not, Gracie? Listen up: 'Gp. Fl (4+1) w25 sec 33m (108ft) 12m. White round tower on house.'" He watched her. "That work for you, captain?" *What's the betting Gracie gets horny in the middle of this?* he thought.

"We take the bay down its centre," she said. Details get her randy. "Punta de Vell coming up, Stephen. I'm certain. There's the light opposite. Check it."

Blackness. Waves smashed at rock.

"Like I said, Gracie. Right at the light."

I strained to see the cliffs I could hear.

"We're too near shore, Stephen. I'm moving out."

The waves were walls, rain driving hard. I grew scared. Gracie fell quiet.

We'd lost sight of the Virgin, our own blue prow.

PARIS INTERLUDE (OCTOBER 1989)

So. I'll yell. In a few minutes, I'm going to yell—I'd decided—I'll yell very loudly and for a long time. Deep breathing in readiness.

We saw It Happened One Night—Claudette Colbert and Clark Gable—in a smoky cinema off Place de La République.

"We're never going to marry, are we Marnie?" I said later in a cheery bar, mirrors trimmed in green and white tile.

You didn't speak.

"That's okay, Marnie."

How could people leave me in here rattling and spluttering? I sat on the toilet, hand on my chin.

"Damn the French."

SAILING WITH GRACIE AND THE EAST SPAIN PILOT (SEPTEMBER 1989)

It seemed like hours. We turned into the Bahia de Cadaqués. Fingers crossed. I was sure I could see the town's lights.

Suddenly, the yacht lurched to one side.

"Wind's changed!" yelled Gracie. "North Easterly! What does the *Pilot* say?"

"We're okay, Gracie. It's gotta be the town ahead. The wind's coming every which way."

"Check the goddam *Pilot*, Stephen."

Holding on, juggling a flashlight, I opened the pages.

"'*Els Vents*,'" I read. "The winds. Eight types of them, Gracie!"

"Which one is this? I can't steer! I can't steer!"

"This is crazy, Gracie. You're doing great. The last gust was '*Gargal*,' northeast."

"Northeast, northeast," she muttered.

Northeast. She steered against it.

"Now it's getting more '*levant*,' east. Or is it '*mestral?*' north west? '*Mestral?*' I know those names. Ponies. Mestral and levant. Horses at a fair! Fuck, Gracie. Do the names matter?"

Gracie slapped me.

PARIS INTERLUDE (OCTOBER 1989)

You held out your finger.

"Hook it," you said. "It's what Irish peasants do. Finger promise."

"What do you promise?" I said, in finger ceremony amongst the mirrors.

"I swear to never trouble you with marriage, Stephen."

"That's a relief," I said. Lying. "What do you tell Lewis?"

"Nothing."

Exactly. That I can believe, Marnie.

What do you tell me?

Idly I tapped my fingernail under the lock. What happened to liberty, fraternity? I wanna know.

SAILING WITH GRACIE AND THE EAST SPAIN PILOT
(SEPTEMBER 1989)

I ducked and grabbed Gracie's arm. We struggled. I meant to stop.
We staggered against the cabins. It happened so quickly. She lost
her footing, fell backwards, but the boat was leaning heavily to that
side. Gracie tumbled like an acrobat into the waves. She fell in.

I hesitated. I really did.

PARIS INTERLUDE (OCTOBER 1989)

Tip-tap. Like notepaper, the mechanism lifted from its envelope.
I gazed at the open door.

"*Up*, you dummy. To get yourself out of this toilet, you lift
the latch up. Up!"

I felt like slamming it shut again.

*"Stephen, I'm too old for this," you said later. Too much cognac at Le
Petit Chateau d'Eau. "I'm sorry, I want to call it quits. I am sorry,
Stephen. I want out."*

This couldn't be right. I stared at the washbasins as though they
were open prairie. *What a clown I am!* How could this have
happened?

SAILING WITH GRACIE AND THE EAST SPAIN PILOT (SEPTEMBER 1989)

For a split second, I thought, "Let her drown." Not because of that day but because of our miserable life together. I had had enough. I savoured the loss, hated it. Her face shaking itself for breath.

"Stephen, help!"

Drowning. How easy.

PARIS INTERLUDE (OCTOBER 1989)

Humming the Marseillaise, I peeped around the door. What if someone had reported a screaming American—distressed, deranged in the washroom?

All clear.

I rushed the door of the universal loo and joined the art-watchers shuffling beyond.

SAILING WITH GRACIE AND THE EAST SPAIN PILOT (SEPTEMBER 1989)

I turned the yacht around. Somehow.

"Stephen!"

I yanked the engine down to a crawl. Tossed the buoy towards her panicked voice.

"Stephen! Help!"

My flashlight tracked her face.

"Here, Stephen! Here!"

I got her back aboard. We made Cadaqués and dropped anchor at Cala Pitxot.

In the morning, Gracie was exhausted and ill. She slept until noon. Her face was cut.

PARIS INTERLUDE (OCTOBER 1989)

The hush of the gallery. The serene, silent enjoyment of it. *I am not myself,* I thought. *Go fuck Lewis, Marnie. You want out?*

When I turned around, a couple of security guards—followed by a pony-tailed man in jeans—were entering the scene of my confinement.

I fled the building. *I can't even get through a lavatory door. I can't get through the simplest thing.*

SAILING WITH GRACIE AND THE EAST SPAIN PILOT
(SEPTEMBER 1989)

In the mirror. There were scratches across my face too. I couldn't remember that happening. I held the glass closer. I stared at caked blood and, beyond, to the giant rocks we'd heard last night.

Clear skies above. The sea—a still, twinkling coyness. I looked from the cut to the blueness alongside my cheek: boats, seagulls. Is that what happened? I gazed at Gracie sleeping. She could be dead. This, a corpse. The day so sunny before us.

Wretched, I turned around to see.

PARIS INTERLUDE (OCTOBER 1989)

What was the matter? You were the matter, Marnie. I'd wanted Gracie to drown. What a coward I am. Was it my story? You needed an out? Can't fuck a killer like me *and* Lewis—someone with intent.

Gracie was alive, and again well—in her bunker back home in Toronto, under Cupid and Venus in Botticelli's *Primavera*: two panels away, and seven more years, from the left-hand-side of the painting where her sleuthing was headed—salvation itself.

Hansel means "gift," you know. I gave you my stories about Gracie. You were a rat—and fled. How could I have let you in on so much?

"Does this make me Gretel?" you said, mocking, in Le Boeuf Sur Le Toit, in that voice, holding out my door-key—my hansel. "You're a woman-hating infant," you told me. "Bring down the walls of Jericho, Stephen."
I'd shown you my soul, offered you another home. I detested you, Marnie.

But I love you, still. I can't help myself. I love you. We're past stories, Marnie. Gretel means "greet." To turn and greet. I'm not gonna let you go, Marnie. I'm not letting go.

III

GALIANO ISLAND, BRITISH COLUMBIA (EARLY MAY 1997)

"Breathe, Stephen. In. Not too hard. That's it."

LEAH'S WEDDING: AN ASIDE (LATE MAY 1997)

"I defy you to write me down," Stephen told a curious author—
"script me out like some bastard 'character.' I defy the words. Any
of them. I go to this wedding—you hear?—because I don't believe
a bloody thing about it. There's only my beautiful daughter to
give away. Beautiful Leah."

GALIANO ISLAND, BRITISH COLUMBIA (EARLY MAY 1997)

"Out."

LEAH'S WEDDING: AN ASIDE (LATE MAY 1997)

"If this is the smell of warm shit, I love it," Stephen told his
author friend. "Part III? Are you kidding? Forget it. The fucking
epilogue, sunshine? Epilogue? No-one writes me off so easily. Nor
you, Leah. Or Gracie, or Marnie, or any of you. Rachel Farber
you understand that. No ending at the end of this story, okay?
No pile of stones—or buttons. Auteur—you listening?"

GALIANO ISLAND, BRITISH COLUMBIA (EARLY MAY 1997)

"In. Gently."

LEAH'S WEDDING: AN ASIDE (LATE MAY 1997)

"I saw us, every one—lost—on art gallery walls. Unfamiliar nudes."

GALIANO ISLAND, BRITISH COLUMBIA (EARLY MAY 1997)

"Out."

RACHEL FARBER (MARCH 1997)

Stephen's stride faltered as he entered the Diane Farris Gallery in Vancouver.

"Stephen!"

Nude, bum-fucking torsos entangled floor to ceiling. Nailed to the walls.

"This-a-way, Stephen!"

Shaved heads, Nazi tattoos, steel-toed boots.

"Rachel! What the hell are you doing here?"

Crowded opening. Men. Marnie's daughter in fashionable boots. White cycle-helmet and saddle in hand. March, 1997.

"Didn't Mom tell you?" I moved here to Vancouver, British Properties, last year."

Everywhere. Men. Jammed in. Sipping champagne.

"I haven't spoken to Marnie in months."

Like the streets and cafés of the Middle East, North Africa. He'd filmed them exhaustively. Now staring at Rachel, he was quickened, hungry.

"I'll be thirty-three soon, Stephen."

Refugee women here and there, like outposts. He thought of Gracie in her Toronto basement—he hadn't seen her in over a year either. That photograph of *Primavera*.

"Already? My daughter Leah's wedding is in May," he said. "It's happening fast."

LEAH'S WEDDING: AN ASIDE (LATE MAY 1997)

"Bare-howling erect."

GALIANO ISLAND, BRITISH COLUMBIA (EARLY MAY 1997)

"Breathe. Let it go. Let it go."

LEAH'S WEDDING: AN ASIDE (LATE MAY 1997)

"Ready?" said Rachel. We walked into the chilly night to her cramped low-rise. Getting close to you again, Marnie. I smelled you on your daughter's breasts. Mackerel. This fresh-faced, blue-eyed woman. "You like older men," I said, as she shoved aside my tie and unbuttoned the shirt. "Call it a spring shower," she replied. "I'm feeling merciful." We knelt on a fake Indian rug. I tasted daughter and mother at my lips.

GALIANO ISLAND, BRITISH COLUMBIA (EARLY MAY 1997)

"Breathe in through your toes."

LEAH'S WEDDING: AN ASIDE (LATE MAY 1997)

"I should tell you something," Rachel said, slipping out of her panties. But I had noticed already. An ostomy bag strapped to her waist—Hollister brand—the size of a small, faithful hand. "Crohn's disease?" She watched me. Her mother's eyes.

GALIANO ISLAND, BRITISH COLUMBIA (EARLY MAY 1997)

"Into your belly, Stephen. Not the chest."

LEAH'S WEDDING: AN ASIDE (LATE MAY 1997)

Ignoring the flesh-coloured pouch, I buried my face between her legs. Harder and harder I ate. I slid into her. My fingers teased her nipples. Over the hot, silky palm. "Deeper," she said, sounding like Marnie. I was loving Marnie. My cock ached with the thrill of them.

GALIANO ISLAND, BRITISH COLUMBIA (EARLY MAY 1997)

"Out through your fingers."

LEAH'S WEDDING: AN ASIDE (LATE MAY 1997)

The giving away is what's left. Taking my Leah's hand and saying, "God bless you, child," and saying, "I'm sorry." Do I do this giving in love or anger? I do it out of horror—of what remains if I don't.

GALIANO ISLAND, BRITISH COLUMBIA (EARLY MAY 1997)

"Don't try so hard. In through your fingers."

LEAH'S WEDDING: AN ASIDE (LATE MAY 1997)

I couldn't stop. Ramming.

RACHEL FARBER (MARCH 1997)

"You heard, then?" said Rachel.

"You're not always the go-between, Rachel. Yeah. This morning. Leah called my hotel. I keep forgetting you and she know one another."

Gracie running the distance back home—the final panel of the famous painting: violets under Mercury's feet. Mercury, the messenger.

"You're passing through?" Rachel said.

What would Gracie see in Attila Lukacs's skinhead boys? Nothing, of course. Gracie stops at the left of Botticelli's canvas.

"Kind of," Stephen said. "I'm scouting for my production company. Leads and more leads. The usual."

Rachel looked away at the walls. *What walls! It's Gracie's life: a final panel.*

"Leah's quite the talent, keeping a wedding secret," he said.

"You don't approve, then, Stephen?"

"I've never met Leah's fiancé."

"His name is Lawrence. Mom's right, Stephen."

"Marnie is?" he said. "About what?"

"You're a kid and a stuffed shirt both. Leah's nineteen. She can decide marriage for herself."

GALIANO ISLAND, BRITISH COLUMBIA (EARLY MAY 1997)

"You're getting it. Breathe for me, Stephen."

LEAH'S WEDDING: AN ASIDE (LATE MAY 1997)

Rachel's eyes. Hands pressed to her hip like Cupid. In prayer.

GALIANO ISLAND, BRITISH COLUMBIA (EARLY MAY 1997)

"Toes, Stephen. Release. Tip-toes out. There we go."

LEAH'S WEDDING: AN ASIDE (LATE MAY 1997)

The ostomy bag broke.

GALIANO ISLAND, BRITISH COLUMBIA (EARLY MAY 1997)

"Breathe."

LEAH'S WEDDING: AN ASIDE (LATE MAY 1997)

"There's no goddamn epilogue, no third part," Stephen said to
the author. "Dickory-dock is what there is. No grasping this. No
grasping anything. So I take my daughter's hand. Give her away—
Leah. Loving her. Because Gracie, you wouldn't. You wouldn't
love your daughter properly. You're right, there is no point to
marriage. Rachel Farber understands that too, don't you? There
is no point. So I come along to Galiano Island and … auteur?
He can't even write *that* down. There's no grasping anything. I
turn my daughter in."

GALIANO ISLAND, BRITISH COLUMBIA (EARLY MAY 1997)

"And rest."

RACHEL FARBER (MARCH 1997)

Stephen spent the first part of 1997, his fortieth year, in a progression of spring seasons: travelling north and west from Bahrain scouting locations for his films about famous artists. Almond blossom, oranges, in Tunis and Malta—January. Irises by the Arno—February.

"Leah's cool," said Rachel.

The longer he drifted, the more he thought of Gracie. Her masterwork.

"How did you meet Leah?"

"My mom introduced us."

In spite and in love, he'd sent Gracie *Primavera* postcards.

"Your *mom*? Marnie introduced you?"

Now. Amidst Lukacs's bum-boys, he pictured Gracie before Botticelli's final panel.

"Your wife had a Christmas bash. We got together."

What else could repressed prairie turn out, thought Stephen—*but a Lukacs? Where do any of us turn—in reaction to our lives?*

"Gracie had a party? You, Leah, Marnie, and Gracie?"

Raging k.d. lang, pursed-rectum Reformers, beef, rednecks, and breathtaking Lukacs—a Basquiat chewing up the wheat fields.

"With Lewis, Mom's man of note, and Lawrence, your daughter's guy."

"So you're going along to Galiano too, in May?"

"I'm Best Woman, Stephen."

"Is Gracie the priest?"

Attila Lukacs's ear-studded, anguished men in their twenties. Bare-assed. "Love in Waiting," "Love in Union"—separation, loss—"Preparing a Bed of Flowers."

"Nah. Leah's not that keen on any of you going, Stephen."

He was itching to film the lives and work of more recent painters. A movie about Attila Lukacs, for example, and his version of *Primavera*—a mirror of Botticelli's painting: carve a swastika onto Cupid.

"That so?"

Give Venus a hard-on and a brush moustache.

"You know why, Stephen."

Strip Zephyrus the wind god, wrap him in red twine.

"Weddings are a dog-and-pony show eh, Rachel?"

Stuff a blue man up Mercury's tunic. What would Gracie say to a painting like that? Would she come to adore Lukacs's art? Three Graces wracked in sexual Lego: Chastity, Faith, and Buggery.

"Leah doesn't 'get' Gracie and you," Rachel said. "But she wants a proper wedding."

GALIANO ISLAND, BRITISH COLUMBIA (EARLY MAY 1997)

Sky rubbed Stephen's earlobes. Fingers, thumbs.

WEDDING: AN ASIDE (LATE MAY 1997)

"Oh fuck!" Rachel cried, gripping my buttocks. Our nostrils flared with the stench. My cock torched. I shot and shot. Collapsing on her body. Scaffolding down. Warm shit. Cut roses. Our panting, sticky bodies.

BRITISH COLUMBIA (EARLY MAY 1997)

His body hummed.

AN ASIDE (LATE MAY 1997)

I ran my hands over the gold of Rachel—and breathed.

(EARLY MAY 1997)

"Take your time," Sky whispered. She slipped from his ear.

(LATE MAY 1997)

Rachel shuddered: first, a giggle.
    Then I sniggered.
    Her stomach shook.

"Shot my load!" she managed to say, wiping her eyes. "What a mess."

Her hand waved in disgust. Like muddied kids—rank, sour, we laughed. Rachel and I on the tufty rug, drying in the glow of street lamps. Soil on our lips. The song of it.

This place of rising—spring.

(MAY 1997)

"See you on the other side, Stephen."

After Queen Zenobia's Telephone

As muezzins chanted sundown call from their Old City minarets, Ian Shaw hurried through the busy Western Temple Gate—with its Corinthian columns and ornamented lintels he had so painstakingly drawn—into the warren of alleys and bazaars that led past Hammam Nureddin to Souq-al-Attarine.

Ian had lost his cellphone—and was late.

Hassan—or "Hazza," as he preferred it—was waiting on Straight Street at the point where Medhet Pasha turns from a covered market of spices and coffee into the huddled lanes of sweets-and-nuts vendors that eventually become Bab Sharqi, the Christian quarter of Old Damascus.

Hazza stood at the water tap on the right, next to a *shawarma* café where at early light a man sold pastries and buns from a cart, distributing five or six to the more starving of the street boys. Hazza finished a cellphone call and sipped mulberry juice from a hawker.

He waved to Ian.

"You climb Mount Qassioun with me tonight," Hazza said. He slung his glass onto the mulberry seller's trolley. "In capital letters"—his way of stressing importance. Conversely, any talk of the U.S. president, the Syrian one, fundamentalism of any stripe, Israel, hip-hop, military service, or September 11th, was "small letters."

"Climb?"

"Yes, of course," he said, primly. "The view is so glorious that even Prophet Mohammed couldn't handle it." Hazza took another phone call; simultaneously he flagged a taxi. "Max, is that you? Ah, *kayfak inta* … how are you, my friend? In capital letters, of course …"

This was Hazza—twenty-two next week. An urgent, generous tour guide who had become Ian's sole friend. They had spent many evenings in sumptuous Old City restaurants. What harm could come to a westerner monitored by the likes of Hazza? A messenger boy whose room in the Bab Touma neighborhood was decked out in yellow "smiley" logos, a giant union jack, postcards of Trafalgar Square, Piccadilly Circus—and a handwritten note above the kitchen doorway, "Mind Your Head."

It was their farewell day. September, 2005. Ian had spent three months painting details of ancient Damascene archways for an architectural firm in Montreal. From his arrival in the teeming, desert city to this traffic-choked dusk in sweltering July heat, he had felt like a child at a fair.

"Why couldn't Mohammed cope?" Ian asked.

"He wished to see Paradise, but at his death."

You shared Hazza's time with a phone-tree of pals, family, acquaintances, Saudis up for the summer, people he had met a minute ago, a year. Clients. It was his way of living, but also ambition. He studied archaeology at the university, yet his passion was to be a tour guide in London, England—at any mention of which his eyes shone brightly, and he would fall uncharacteristically mute as though Paradise itself lay within reach.

Like many Syrians, he secretly wanted to flee Syria—and, like them too, had been refused a visa. His daily conduct helped him forget that he might never escape. A North American in tow felt like compensation, he told Ian. Hazza behaved haughtily and with defiance towards a State that had crossed him.

Hazza and Ian hopped into a cab.

"My wife has your cellphone number," Ian reminded him from the front seat between calls, as the tiny cab weaved and honked through the bedlam of central Damascus in the direction of the mountain slopes. "Jessica's meeting me at the Montreal airport tomorrow evening. She will no doubt call your phone. My own number's lost."

"The countdown has begun," Hazza said. "In the morning you'll leave, and I'll be without a cherished friend."

"I'll miss you."

"She must be the queen of wives to telephone so far."

"Jessica *is*," Ian said. "A thousand times queen."

Hazza rolled his eyes. More at the fact, it seemed, that the car's engine was not really up to a steep, unlit hill, at night. He tapped the driver's shoulder and pretended annoyance.

"I told this gentleman his taxi is a donkey," Hazza said, from the backseat. "He should pay *us* a hundred Syrian pounds to ride in it."

The driver laughed. A young, cheeky passenger behind. Gullible alien in front. Hazza reached over and turned up the radio. He began clicking his fingers, gyrating, to a popular, modern singer, Fairuz.

"*Salaam-alaykum,*" Ian said to the driver, one of his few Arabic greetings—used habitually, if somewhat belatedly, every time he took a cab and felt at ease. It meant "peace be upon you," which was a bit solemn for his taste.

Ian's intent was, "I'm glad to meet you and am now comfortable, I can't speak a word more, please don't injure me with your driving in this disorganized city or rip me off, seeing as I've finally made an effort to speak." It was lot to cram into "hello"—but it invariably landed him a handshake and friendly nod, if no discount.

"*Ismi* Ian," he went on valiantly. My name is Ian.

"Salah!" from the driver. He clapped the air jubilantly. To the music. Or the sound of Arabic from a newcomer's lips. The car slowed to a snail's pace, the incline severe. What did it matter if there was dancing in this petite, shuddering shell of a deathtrap? "Sala*din*."

Ian assumed this was his name—Salah or Saladin. Most Muslim men seemed to have a shortened name and wanted you to use it—like Ian's saying "hello" and meaning a litany, always with a view to comprehending more, offering goodwill, protecting himself.

Ian nodded gratefully—wishing Salah would steer with at least one hand on the wheel, rather than a knee. The guy, applauding, was more engrossed by his rear-view mirror than by traffic overtaking on this potholed road—or the westerner's drivel. Not every passenger tried disco *seated*, it seemed. The driver was enthralled.

Salah turned the volume higher and grinned. Hazza had this effect on people. He could belly-dance to Umm Kolthum, Madonna, the Backstreet Boys, or Sting. You name it, the lad had a move. Salah was ecstatic and began to croon with the radio, urging Ian to move his legs, do something. Keep the dancer company.

Ian wound down the window and tapped on the door. Music streamed out amidst a cacophony of horns, revving engines. It was Friday evening. To Hazza, this day had not involved prayers but sleep in preparation for a night at The Backdoor with his girlfriend Fernanda, a seventeen-year-old Lebanese-Brazilian. Orphan, model. She celebrated Hazza's flamboyant ways. The couple enjoyed free entry to the uptown clubs—drinks—and were *the* spectacle from midnight until dawn, so Hazza said. They cavorted—lost themselves in strobe light.

Every Friday, he and Fernanda invited Ian. The Canadian declined. Tonight, his last, the party-pooper accepted. There was nothing to lose. His flight was 6:00 AM. Why not stay awake, partying at Damascus's hottest club?

This was the grand holiday of each week. "Friday-the-Smiley," Hazza called it. Families picnicked on traffic islands, on the slopes of Mount Qassioun, along roadsides, to flee the pollution and heat of the lower city. Total, unforgiving celebration—in the dark.

Three months before, Ian shunned these locales. *Any* crowds, in fact, nightspots, traffic jams—wherever he felt closed in. Public holidays. Friday noon prayers—occasions to avoid. The travel advisories said so. You remained in your digs. Ian's imagination was fuelled by alarm: of abduction, Syrian spies, rendition, torture, decapitation, the odd suicide bomber.

Not surprisingly, the Quebec company paid him handsomely for his drawings. An assignment too unpredictable for most—with Iraq a stone's throw away, and Baghdad. Most people did not risk life and limb for historic, decorated porticos. On edge still, though—in these closing hours Ian tried to savour the unpredictable. No-one meant any ill will. Quite the opposite. Why could he not feel that—benevolence?

Ian needed even more time—to appreciate what living here *meant*. Why, in his mid-thirties, was he so exhilarated, frightened?

Inspired? Three months had taken him far past the novelty of Damascus, and Syrians.

"We travel up there!" Hazza said. He pointed to terrace lights on the distant hill as Salah swerved to avoid a trench.

"Is it better than the Palmyra oasis?" Ian asked.

No reply.

Ian glanced over his shoulder.

It was one of those instances when Hazza fell silent—as at the mention of London, England. There was sadness in his eyes, apprehension. Hazza squirmed and clicked his fingers harder to Fairuz.

On this last night, Ian should not have mentioned the previous week's trip east to the second-century ruins of Palmyra, and the desert camel journey, the stay with a Bedouin family near Iraq's border. It had affected them both—and brought their friendship closer to love.

On the day their four-camel convoy lit out past the citadel and east towards the Euphrates river, Hazza recited a history of the palm-fringed city—the Temple of Bel, the legendary Queen Zenobia of ancient Roman times.

In a Palmyra hotel, he once offered a cumbersome rotary phone to a Japanese tourist who irritated him. Hazza called it "Queen Zenobia's Telephone."

"Her majesty would dial from Palmyra?" the fellow from Tokyo said, poking his finger into the third-century dial. "To Emperor Aurelian?"

"Flat rates to Rome," Hazza said.

The man, of course, wished to purchase it immediately. He had bought a "flying" carpet, after all, from an equally canny Syrian in the Hamidiyyah souq in Damascus. Hazza professed little time for ignorant visitors. Ian himself barely escaped Hazza's insistence that foreigners be knowledgeable about Syria, plugged in minimally to the country's history and culture. Ian had fallen afoul of Hazza's reminder that the Ummayyad mosque in Old Damascus was where Isa would return at "The End of Days."

"Who is Isa?" Ian asked.

"It's Jesus," replied Hazza. "You freak of a man."

In the desert, under a starlit sky—before a goat-hair tent— Hazza and the Bedouin family patiently, ceremoniously, taught Ian Arabic numerals.

"*Ashara, tis'a, tamanya,*" they said in chorus.

Ten, nine, eight, he repeated in their tongue.

Hazza seemed to revel in it and, in spite of no cellphone signal, the sweet tea and cakes. He and Ian slept outside, on carpets, under a canopy of planets. Hazza with his Canadian friend, holding Ian's hand.

"Westerners stand on the shores of things," Hazza said, that night. "I'm fascinated how you struggle to live."

In return for numeracy lessons, Ian contributed to the Bedouins' amusement at rhyme and catchy phrases. "See you later, alligator," they adored and repeated. "Bees knees, willy woofter, cat's whisker."

Next afternoon, as the camels transported them under a blistering sun, Ian rehearsed his class of the previous night. Hazza corrected him against the wind-borne sand.

"*Saba'a, sitta,*" seven, six.

"Bee's knees!" Hazza sang out. "A gold star for Ali Baba."

On the return to Palmyra from the desert—and when he was not humming Madonna songs or reciting poetry by

Al-Mutanabbi—Hazza reminded Ian of the five pillars of Islam. Named the five prayer times in a day. Much was about numbers, it seemed, in Hazza's world. Ian was instructed—wiggled his sunburned fingers and toes to the count.

Ian left the desert vowing to return, stay longer.

"Do you remember your numbers?" Hazza yelled above the music in the taxi. He looked angry.

They were nearing the crest of Mount Qassioun—Damascus below, its green minarets like missile quills.

"Five, four, three, two, one?" said Ian.

"You learned them forwards as well, right?"

Ian nodded—and felt concern that Hazza seemed so upset. This boy was proud and accomplished. An Alawite. His minority sect now dominated Syria's sixteen-million Sunnis. The rulers were from Hazza's tribe, based in the hills around Latakia where his family lived.

Hazza was Syria—at least in Ian's eyes. Even though Hazza wished to escape the country, he also wanted visitors, and people like Ian, to see and feel—as fervently as he did. As Syrians did. Intensely, holding nothing back.

"*Khamsa, arba'a, talaata,*" Ian piped up. Five, four, three. "*Itnayn, waHid.*"

Strains of desert Bedouin, not easily forgotten

Then another call on Hazza's cell.

"For you," he said, tossing Ian his phone.

It was Jessica.

"Hi, honey … I lost my BlackBerry … yeah …"

The cab lurched to avoid yet another pit in the summit road. This time, the jolt dislodged a carton of purple tissues somehow affixed to the roof above Salah's dashboard. It tumbled onto Ian's bare arm. The corner pierced his skin and knocked the cellphone from his hand.

"Hey!" A startled Ian slammed against the door as though he'd been hit.

Hazza wrenched the driver's shoulder so that he would brake. Ian scrambled under the seat to reach his wife.

Locating the cell, he pressed it hard against his ear.

"It's okay, Jessica. Everything's fine," he said. "We're in a cab. I dropped Hazza's phone ..."

The driver's steering wobbled for a few metres before the cab resumed its course. Salah seemed shaken by the hullabaloo—pulled over and turned off the radio.

"The guide I told you about ... yes, up a mountain ..."

Hazza scrambled into the darkness for a leak. He wandered the curbside—plucked a flower from the verge, strolled in a grove of cedars.

As Hazza reached the taxi, Ian handed him the cell. "Jessica wants to say hi."

In the backseat, Hazza listened good-humouredly to Ian's wife. He waved the driver to move on. Hazza frowned, grinned, by turns—as though he spoke daily to Montrealers like Jessica. Ian could not take his eyes off Hazza, whose expression became serene, as though someone had uttered "London" in his ear.

"Your husband was attacked by a violet tissue box, Mrs. Jessica," he said eventually, as though it needed explaining.

Hazza loved gags. Ian recalled his mimicry of worked-up foreigners visiting Syria.

Salah lit two Marlboros and offered one to Ian who, still in the front seat, was amused by the heart shape of Salah's tissue-box holder above his head.

"Yes," Hazza said to Jessica. He laughed, pulled a face. His eyes grew teary with mischief. Hazza booted the driver's elbow to turn on the radio. "Travel is extremely treacherous in Damascus."

The driver fumbled for the volume.

"No, Mrs. Jessica he will DANCE ALL NIGHT," Hazza said. He twisted a jasmine petal and sniffed into the silver mouthpiece. "Flat rates to Montreal."

Ian glanced over his shoulder at his friend and turned back to face the mountain peak. Slowly, Ian drew on his cigarette and blew rings into the windscreen: two, one, zero.

"*Sifr*," he told Salah wistfully. Moonlit pebbles upon the glass. "*Itnayn, waHid, sifr*."

"Come morning, I will kill him," from the backseat.

"Dog Stare" was published in *The Dalhousie Review* (2013). "Dotty" and "An Island in the South Pacific" appeared in *Grain Magazine* (2010, 2006). "After Queen Zenobia's Telephone" was published in *The Antigonish Review* (2007). "Seriously" and "Face" were both shortlisted for the CBC Literary Awards (2006)—the former was published in the U.S. in *Leaf Garden* (2010) and was a finalist in the Sheldon Currie Fiction Contest (2009); the latter was published in the U.S. in *DREAMScene.* "More Than Anyone on Earth" and "You Turn Your Back" appeared in 2003, in *The Antigonish Review* (as "Unmentionable") and *Descant*, respectively. "You Turn Your Back" was a finalist in the *Prism International* Annual Short Story Contest (1996). "¿Who Knows Where?" was published in an abridged form in *Queen Street Quarterly* (2001), and unabridged in *The New Quarterly* (2002). "Primavera"—with the title "Hands Over the Body"—was a finalist in the U.S. New Century Writer Awards (2002) and a segment, entitled "Redwater," won the Chapters Prize in *Blood and Aphorisms: New Writing* (1998). "Blanks" appeared as "Crooked Hollow" in *Blood and Aphorisms: New Writing* (1995) and won the Fiction Prize in the Annual Literary Awards (Hamilton and Region Arts Council). The stories have been revised.

ACKNOWLEDGEMENTS

I would like to thank my friends and colleagues who offered encouragement as this work evolved. In particular, I am grateful to Bethany Gibson, Jean Van Loon, Susan Swan, Patrick Lane, Vivette Kady, and the late Timothy Findley, for their editorial eyes. At Tightrope, Dawn Kresan for her typographical and design skills; Heather Wood and Deanna Janovski, for their tremendous support. Rosa Regàs, Anna Omedes, and Federico Montagud, for their friendship and inspiration. The Hawthornden Literary Institute, Banff Centre for the Arts, and Danish Cultural Institute (Damascus) for welcome surprises and uninterrupted time. I am indebted to Audrey Thomas for a stay at her beautiful studio on Galiano Island, British Columbia, and to Louise Doddrell for time at Alcana, Spain. Lei Zhao, Lorna Dunn, Marsha McDonald, Heather Kays, Leanne Forsythe, Jim Nason and Don Smith, Chris Boyd, Bernard Trossman, Sam Auron, and Brandon Thornton are much-loved, fellow travellers. The Canada Council for the Arts, Ontario Arts Council, and Toronto Arts Council have stood, repeatedly, at my back.